MURDER...
THE ASHES OF
NASS BEACON

by

A. K. Oakes-Odger MBE

Grosvenor House
Publishing Limited

This book is published by
Grosvenor House Publishing Ltd
28-30 High Street, Guildford, Surrey, GU1 3EL.
www.grosvenorhousepublishing.co.uk

A CIP record for this book
is available from the British Library

ISBN 978-1-78148-345-9

This book is dedicated to the memory of my beloved Son Westley J.B. Odger born 18th August, 1978. During the writing of this book he was brutally murdered on the 12th September, 2005.

Westley J.B. Odger

Proceeds from the sale of this book will be donated to our Charity in memory of Westley Odger. The monies will help to continue our work with families affected by Murder and Manslaughter. Our wide range of services, include peer support, advocacy and training. Monies raised will also help fund our work in Schools, Colleges and Universities.

Prince of Tides 'Westley Odger' Foundation
www.KnifeCrimes.Org

This book is also dedicated to Westley's much loved Brother Lee and Sister Rachael and my granddaughter, Chloe.

To my brother, William and to our mother, Gladys Victoria…the light of this family's lives; To the memory of my father, William Henry Oakes, an extraordinary man who served during the Second World War as a No. 4 Commando. His gallantry and that of his comrades inspired the telling of this story and that of the factual events of the No. 4 Commando raids.

On the 21st May, 1948 the Rt. Hon. Sir Winston L.S. Churchill unveiled The Commando Memorial at Westminster Abbey. On the 16th September, 1957 Her Majesty, The Queen approved the award of the following battle honours to The Commando Association in recognition of the services of the Commandos in the Second World War:-

"Vaagso," "Norway, 1941," "St. Nazaire" "Dieppe," "Normandy Landings," "Dives Crossing," "Flushing," "Westkapelle," "Rhine," "Leese," "Aller," "North-West Europe, 1942, '44-45," "Litani," "Syria, 1941," "Steamroller Farm," "Sedjenane I," "Djebel Choucha," "North Africa, 1941-43," "Landing in Sicily," "Pursuit to Messina," "Sicily, 1943," "Landing at Porto San Venere," "Termoli," "Salerno," "Monte Ornito," "Anzio," "Valli di Comacchio," "Argenta Cap," "Italy, 1943-45," "Greece, 1944-45," "Crete," "Madagascar," "Adriatic," "Middle East, 1941, '42, '44," "Alethangyaw," "Kangaw," "Burma, 1943-45."

The Battle of Honours for No. 4 Commando are:-

"Lofoten Islands (Norway), 1941," "Boulogne, 1942," "Dieppe, 1942," "Normandy Landings,"

"D-Day, 1944," "Dives Crossing," "Flushing,"
"North-West Europe, 1944-45."

The Commando Association Battle Honours Flag was
dedicated in Westminster Abbey, 15th April, 1961.
On Saturday, 1st May, 1971 my family were honoured
to be invited by the Commando Association to attend
the Service of Thanksgiving at the Laying Up of the
Battle Honours Flag of the Commando Association in
the presence of Her Majesty, Queen Elizabeth the
Queen Mother.

The Battle of Honours Flag was unveiled by
Her Majesty in its final home in
St. George's Chapel, Westminster Abbey.

A beautifully inscribed Commando Roll of Honour
Book can also be seen in St. George's Chapel,
containing the names of 1,706 ex-Commando
Soldiers, Army and Royal Marine, who lost their
lives during the 1939-45 War.

Introduction

The most interesting things in life often happen by accident. That is how Anneka found herself experiencing the passions, wild times, friendship and loss. Success and more money than any one person can spend. Roused by one single act of violence Margot murders the one man she loves...the chilling realisation, drives her take her own life. In the brilliant dark-hued mysteries of the gender wars, is a haunting love story

When Anneka meets Willie Flynn...this story charts the journey of growing up in the

East End of London during the Second World War... through the 1950's hardships, to the 'Swinging Sixties'.

The strong-willed and excessive nature of Willie Flynn and the determination and grit of Anneka makes for an explosive relationship that comes full circle from a War of attrition

Both characters are extraordinary people from extraordinary backgrounds. Their meeting to change their lives and destiny forever during an extraordinary time in history

World War Two...

Chapter One

It was around two o'clock in the afternoon...a sweltering hot and sticky, July day. There's never enough time in this hectic lifestyle these days, for self-indulgence; I'd done most of the daily chores...plenty more to do but, hey "damn it" I said out loud "*Carpe Diem*". Leaving the few bits of washing up from lunch, I marched myself into the kitchen and, taking the largest glass I could find, filled it with ice and lemonade. Then rushed off upstairs, climbed into a bikini, grabbed the sunscreen, a book, then out into the secluded garden and settled myself onto a large towel on the lawn. Yes... I thought, I may as well 'seize the day'...these summers in England are too unpredictable to miss out on such a glorious bit of sunshine. That's my excuse, best I could find, and it would do very nicely, thank you. A quiet Saturday, so far, so good, not even a 'phone call? Makes a change I chuckled...perhaps too good to be true, better make the most of it. Oh! Please don't let the 'phone ring...

Sipping the cool lemonade whilst opening the book and noticing that there didn't seem to be many birds about today? Perhaps it's too hot, although I could just hear the beautiful sound of a 'song thrush' coming from somewhere. How different life seems on a summer's day, the air, the smells, even the same noises, sound somehow different...everything more colourful! The garden's so beautiful now, today especially, transformed from the once desolate plot that it was when I moved here 10 years ago. Just a wire mesh fence around the boundaries, lumps of concrete, bricks and bits of builders' rubble, clay and plenty of weeds. The conifers, the first to be planted, are now well established forming a complete screen around the whole garden, the lawn also lush and green with various shaped sections that include different fruit trees, shrubs and tropical plants. Other shaped areas have roses and bedding plants. Towards the house, near the patio, the ornamental pond is overlooked by a life-sized statue of a man holding an urn, from which water cascades into the pond. Also, there's a separate fountain in the middle of the pond and the trickling sounds from each inter-mingle, adding to the ambience of this perfectly peaceful day. The resulting serenity is broken only by the odd delightful screams of children having fun somewhere in the distance, a whirring of someone mowing their lawn and the occasional muffled drone of an aeroplane, as it makes its way invisibly overhead. I looked around with self-satisfaction at the 'garden room' as I call it and thought, 'there's really nothing about it I would change!' Whilst this thought is pleasing, I was aware of being disappointed at the same time...'it is nice to change things, sometimes!'

Last year I had put an Arbour in the centre of the garden, on its three ornamental wrought iron sides I'd planted roses called 'Peace'. They had climbed nicely, their pinkish-yellow blooms wafting a strong perfumed aroma around the garden, to herald their presence.

Also included is a large, old fashioned Victorian style solar light in the centre, which looks rather like the street lamps see in a history book depicting 'Victorian Times'. This light is hung at the highest point of the Arbour, the other matching lights are around the patio, the pond and in the trees. Each night at dusk, the lights gently become brighter, keeping the garden alive 'til daybreak. Over in the far corner of the garden I'd erected a raised wooden terrace with stairs up to a seating area, enclosed by carved balustrades. It's hexagonal shape...complete with roof, making it look like a band stand, giving rise to some jokes of course...such as, 'where's the brass band?' Truthfully, it was made that way quite deliberately...it reminds of the band stand in Victoria Park, in London, where I used to live. There's trellis at the back, just behind the 'mock band stand' supporting sweet smelling honeysuckle and no doubt, plenty of spiders! Some of the other trellised sections around the garden have differing varieties of passion flowers. At this time of the year, having already sent out their spindled feelers, which had entwined around everything they'd come into contact with...now beginning to open their flowers.

I noticed the haunting sounds from the large bamboo wind chime becoming more frequent feeling grateful for the soothing, cool breeze which stopped this heat from being unbearable. This wind chime is hanging on the veranda, which is on the opposite corner of the garden, from the terrace. I closed my eyes momentarily...'yes!' I thought, 'those sounds reminds me of the Far East, peaceful images of Buddhist Monks in worship, places like Tibet, Thailand or...somewhere up in the Mountains, perhaps even in the Thamkrabok Monastery itself!' Opening my eyes again suddenly, with feelings of guilt...

I should really be doing something, not daydreaming! Stupid perhaps but, I so rarely do 'self-indulgent laziness, that I no longer know how to enjoy it!' Getting absolutely nowhere, with the book, I threw it down, glancing back at the same time to take in a quick inspection of the grapevines. They had now grown all the way up the large wooden uprights, and over the cross sections, leading from the side of the veranda, which formed a walkthrough of around thirty vines, to the ivy-clad arched back gate, keeping the rest of the world from sight. Looking good, I thought, taking great delight in the fact that they would actually yield usable grapes this year! Wonderful!

A seductive aroma was now seeping into my senses... making me feel quite hungry...someone's having a barbecue, the smell is simply delicious. Barbecued food and a glass of Chardonnay, or better still Champagne would be really the 'icing on the cake' right now, I smiled. Still, that's out ...having done the 'drinking for England' in the past, with great 'gusto' at every impromptu party or indeed any occasion that might justifiably warrant the 'turning up of the bottle' ceremony, had decided it had to stop! So, gave up the demon drink! This really is another story.

This momentous decision was aided and indeed, I have to admit, prompted by an incident at a party. The girl involved to whom I guess, I owe some 'thanks?' The event, I chuckled, had to happen at the 'event of the year' of course, about 4 years ago now. It was whilst at the Grand Annual Ball, held in the Officer's Club at the Colchester Garrison. A big event, attended by, high ranking Officers, their wives or girlfriends and other important guests. Also the 'usual suspects' of Colchester's social elite of notable wealth and title, including the

Mayor, the locally elected MP, hoteliers and so on, and so forth...all of which, included myself! All dignitaries present had been sent 'Private Invitations' only. The girl in question, who's name I can't recall, was to my mind of the rather 'bitchy type!' A 'well endowed' blonde dressed to kill, wearing a low-cut, long and clinging 'flame red' evening dress. She...the girl in question...having developed a thought in her mind, that I was after 'her man' (a ridiculous idea – it's just not my style, and 'he' certainly wasn't my type), began shouting across the crowded hall, to the utter dismay of everyone. Hurling verbal abuse with notable venom and in a state of 'green-eyed' jealousy, her melodious cursing turning all heads in the room. I quickly became aware that the torrent of verbal expletives directed at me...

"keep your hands off...you bleep, bleep, lush!"

Even in my delightfully inebriated state, immediately recognised the title of 'lush' as being anything but 'a compliment!' It was the sort of 'classic' situation that one sniggers at seeing someone else in but, 'Oh! My God' it was happening to me! Looking around the room at the 'open mouthed' guests awaiting my reaction, I was duly indignant! I certainly wasn't after 'her' man! I usually had difficulty dealing with my own man, let alone someone else's, although she may have a point about the drinking?

Engaging 'mouth before brain' in a desperate attempt to save some dignity, made the situation all the worse with my retort...

"So sorry Ma'am, I forgot to bring my glasses!"

This instantly caused her to puff up in red-faced anger, at the seemingly huge insult to her man (which really wasn't my intention). The frozen faces, now took a sharp intake of breath, then luckily for me no doubt, all burst into laughter! Phew...situation deflated. As for my gaff, what can I say? The rest of the evening went on to be very enjoyable, but I secretly made a promise to myself...'things had to change, drinking had to go1' I've kept that promise, from that day, which reminds me, with a jolt back to reality...'I'm thirsty '.

Going back indoors to the kitchen, opening the fridge to view the contents, decided, that in order for the day to be enjoyed in true and absolute decadence required the preparation of some smoked salmon with lemon, perhaps a little paprika, salad, and brown bread. Oh! Yes! I think I'll have those strawberries too, topped with cream. I laid a tray with the 'mouth-watering' delights, continuing to 'twist in my sobriety' with a glass of cold cranberry juice! Then, back into the garden to make myself comfortable again. I guess I'm at that age when the body becomes more of a 'temple' as opposed to an 'amusement park!' Suppose I can't complain...at the advancing years...having enjoyed to the full, the bright lights and a ride on the carousel of life with few regrets? I'd dyed my hair every imaginable colour for so many years that I couldn't remember the real colour, until finally growing it out, quite recently? Had many different hairstyles too, including the 'avant-garde'...it's a wonder really, that it's still thick and dark. I now wear it in a simple I'm informed, trendy style. For most of my life, I was told that I was too thin, however, it was fine with me, in fact, I was still wearing size 10 clothes until well into my 50's...when suddenly my bra-less lifestyle changed? An absolute absurdity, in my humble opinion, to develop 'curves' of the feminine sort, need to wear a bra' and wiggle when I walk, whether I like it or not, at an age when it's not needed? Being now a size 12/14 is quite good, I suppose? Guess it's true 'being fuller is better' after all Marilyn Monroe was a size 16, or so it's reported, I find that hard to believe? Perhaps it's propaganda and secret lies…but, everyone says

"You look so much better these days, especially now you've put on some weight?"

'I still get a 'chat-up' occasionally' I thought reassuringly …but, it's still a 'bugger' on the pocket! The wonderful 'classic style' clothes in the wardrobe with designer labels belong to another person, I chuckled! I still recognise the woman I see when I look in the mirror…just? In devilish humour gave a 'laugh' out loud! Yes! But what will happen in another 10 or 20 years' time…will I look in the mirror and say

"Who the hell is that?"

Really and truthfully I'm not overly concerned with ageism, it's a waste of emotion. I'm active and always exercise, eat well, with a mentally youthful and fairly liberated attitude to life. I don't think I'm the type to 'go under the knife' but, hey-ho 'never, say never!' It's great not to worry anymore about whether people 'like' me or 'not' or that I can't be seen in public without my 'make-up' (although, I still like to get my 'body up' each morning). Nor, do I concern myself with any other unnecessary 'stuff', as I did in years past.

I remember the misery I'd experienced when I started my very first job which incidentally, was as a 'GPO Telephonist, considered then to be a really 'good job?'

For the first week, not a soul would speak to me? I'd walk into the Telephone Exchange 'switch-room' wearing the large black 'Bakelite head-set' with its dangling cable and 'jack-plug' whilst dramatically 'tossing' my head in the air. I'll show them I'm not bothered by having been sent to Coventry! This 'head-tossing' was not an easy task, as the cumbersome equipment was very heavy, uncomfortable and looked quite ridiculous, now I think of it? It consisted of a large oval 'ear-phone' - worn on one ear, which was attached to a sort of head-band, made of thin metal! Connected to this 'ear-phone' was a huge 'black trumpet' affair that one spoke in to. Of course, my defiant 'air of superiority' and over the top 'body language' suitably confirmed their view...that I was a complete snob, 'should be taken down a peg'....'who does she think she is, Royalty?'

I smiled at this memory as the thought flashed across my mind...'I wonder where all those girls are now?' Thinking about and realising I'd probably brought some of their attitude upon myself, as I'd always appeared far too 'Ten Gallon' and 'Gung-Ho'! How silly it all seems now! I'm certainly not so sensitive anymore but, as for 'Gung-Ho' if I'm being honest, well, you know the saying 'old dogs, new tricks?' However, I'd rather say I'm passionate about different and more important issues.

Luckily...still holding plenty of dreams, aspirations and goals but, it's not to prove anything to anyone else, the aim purely personal achievement. From this point of view, it's a good time of life...I'm never going to be a 'Little House on the Prairie' or 'Woman's Guild' type, that's for sure! Hopefully, this 'fire in the belly' with burn for plenty a year yet! I'll be happy with a 100th Birthday Cake, anything after that is 'a bonus' I mussed! Whilst, I'm giving myself 'brownie points' I should also feel fortunate that I've not become cynical, as some people I know...just hold a healthy realism to what is going on around me! I suddenly pulled myself up with a jolt...

'you'd better stop this line of thought before you become compelled to go out and be seriously bad?'

My attention, suddenly drawn to the searing pain in my leg...Ouch! Slapping at the large insects attacking me and cursing...'Bloody horrible things!'

It was difficult to feel any sympathy at the demise of the poor squashed creatures, as the bite lumps were appearing in several places! How long could I resist the urge to scratch at them? It's still such a beautiful afternoon, but that time of the day, when midges and other creepy-crawlies come out to eat unsuspecting humans! I picked up my book and tried to read again without success! I maybe relaxing the body, but my mind felt like a 'washing machine' back and forth, back and forth! Wondering this, pondering that? Times...people...places!

"Oh! Look at that"

I said aloud, suddenly noticing a pair of 'Blue Tits' flying from one tree to another, playfully. I watched them for a while before I laid down, closed my eyes again to become sleepy and dreamlike...'it's wonderful to live here, but I will always miss London' I sighed...drifting into fond memories of my childhood. Aware now of thinking back...back, and further back, and wondering how far my memory would allow? What are my earliest memories of childhood

Chapter Two

I was surprised to find I could recall standing in my cot, gripping the sides! Screaming frantically, desperately trying to climb out? Amazing, the reality of this vivid memory, decades later still so perfectly preserved, and still conjures a real sense of fear! These clear recollections filled with terror, still so haunting and emotional, the shadows of half-light creating huge threatening shapes over Mother's face, as she lay in bed. It was probably only a short time of sending out the despairing sobs, before she came to comfort me, and quite why I was so afraid is lost to me now, but it was Wartime!

I was born in the early hours of the 8th day of February, 1941 in the terraced house of No. 7 Cantrell Road, Bow, in the East End of London, the home of my maternal grandparents, George and Ann Symmonds. It was, in those days, still home also to Mum's three brothers and one sister, as well as great auntie May. Mum and Dad, many months before my birth had already chosen names. A boy would be called William, according to family tradition on Dad's side, for generations the first born son being named 'William'. A girl would be Anneka, as I came to be known, a

Hebrew word for 'grace'. This was my mother's choice, an unusual name she'd always liked, from her side of the family. When old enough to acknowledge this name, I'd thought this choice very strange, "why couldn't I have been a Jane or Sylvia or something more ordinary 'I'd moan'. Upon learning its origin, went on to become boringly boastful, by telling anyone who'd listen! It's a Scandinavian name...and the story goes, that back in our family history on my mother's side, of sea-faring Naval men, one of her ancestral Grandfathers' had reputedly met, fell in love with and married, a 'well known' Scandinavian actress called Anneka. Anneka... was the daughter of a wealthy merchant, who had reluctantly given my Great, Great, Great Grandfather, his daughter's hand in marriage. Later, they'd returned to England, settled somewhere in Norfolk, and went on to have a large family. I've often thought of research-ing the family genealogy to find out more, perhaps it explains my somewhat flamboyant attitudes? Like many families of different geographic peoples' make-up, there's also a heavy Irish influence, again on my mother's side. But, sadly, not too much is known about my father's 'blood' origins, other than he had a very distinctive 'Italian' appearance! We know his forefathers were mostly in the Military, and lived in the Norfolk area, in the early part of the 17th Century, a fact I've always thought strangely coincidental. Whilst, I seem to have inherited Father's colouring of dark hair, olive skin, although with blue eyes; to my great annoyance I've not inherited his beautiful singing voice. My brother William, who was to follow my arrival 13 months later, is the walking double of dad with the exception of being 'fair haired' and of course...inherited his beautiful 'voice'. Although, he doesn't sing he speaks with the same rounded precise, velvet smooth tones…which, I might add has caused many a girl to 'swoon over' especially when he speaks on the telephone!

Father had joined-up into the Army like his father before him, which happened to coincide with the Second World War. Later, he volunteered for Special Service and successfully became a No. 4 Commando.

Mum and Dad met when 'fate played a hand' and 'Cupid's Arrow' struck them whilst at the boating lake, in London's 'Victoria Park.' It was the summer of 1939 just before the start of the War, a couple of months later. Mum had taken her young brother, John to the park for the day and he'd wanted to go on a rowing boat. Dad had taken out a rowing boat at around the same time, having gone to the park with his sister, Sally. Dad and Sally had spent the earlier part of the day rehearsing, as he was due to perform that evening, singing at a Dinner Dance. Dad's singing voice was good enough to have been professional, sounding not unlike Mario Lanza, even later in life. He'd been heard by someone from the BBC on one occasion, and went on to perform on the radio a number of times. Even if the War hadn't happened, I'll never know whether he'd ever wanted to turn professional. I'd wondered, but never got around to asking him. Mum, an accomplished 'machinist' made tailored suits, but at the start of the War went on to war work, making aeroplane wings! I cannot imagine how she could have done this kind of work…she was hardly built for it?

Accidentally, and possibly on purpose, his boat had collided with the boat mum was in. He quickly 'seized the moment' offering to buy Mum and young John an 'ice-cream' by way of an apology...he'd wait at the ice-cream stand, nearby? Before Mum could answer, young John said...

"Oh, yes please Sir, thank you!"

They met up, as arranged, sitting by the lake and chatting whilst eating their 'ice-creams'. Having introduced each other, Dad went on to explain how he'd come to be at the park, and invited Mum to the Dance.

"You'll have company, Sally will be there!"

He'd confirmed, already captivated by mother's obvious beauty!

"I could collect you, and naturally, bring you home... please say you'll come?"

From the moment Mum had met his gaze, she'd thought, 'He looks just like Ronald Coleman...even speaks like him'. Ronald Coleman was Mum's screen idol!

Mum wanted to accept, instantly, whilst...feeling concerned she may appear, too eager? "Well, OK...I'll have to get my parents' permission."

Giving him the address and instructing him!

"When you arrive, you'll have to be formally introduced!"

"Of course, that's fine" he'd replied, wearing a broad grin that lit his whole face.

"It's a date then...see you at around 7pm."

"Yes!" She'd replied.

Temporarily, they parted to go in separate directions, 'til later. Mum, meanwhile feeling anxious and wondering how it would be received at home, 'would she be allowed to go?' Then she became flustered when thinking to herself...'if it's agreed to, will her two older brothers, George and Bill, be dispatched to follow her and spy?' This was very possible as they'd done it before; even if she'd only gone out for an evening in a foursome with her sister Ann (nicknamed 'Cissy' by brother George), it was their usual 'trick?

Once, Mum had gone to the pictures with a lad named Alfie, who lived close by. Mum's parents, knew his parents, so she was allowed to go. About halfway through the film Alfie, rather cheekily, had slid his arm around her shoulder...almost immediately, Mum heard him shout out...

"Ouch!"

He'd received a sharp 'slap' on the back of his head, accompanied by the words...

"Steady there, Alfie...what do you think you're doing...that's our sister you're 'making-up' to...?"

Sat in the two seats, of the row immediately behind, was mum's brothers, George and Bill. Alfie, took his arm away faster than a 'bullet leaves a gun'... sitting as stiff as a board for the duration, 'til the end of the film.

Dad arrived to collect Mum for the dance as arranged at 7pm, to Mum's despair, minus his sister Sally? He was duly escorted in to the front parlour by Mum's parents, then no doubt 'grilled' until they were satisfied of his honourable intent! Mother listening, outside the door with bated breath! Needless to say, Mum was allowed on the date; she wore her very best dress. I can still hear Dad's voice now, with his infectious 'chuckle' as he spoke of how they'd met. He'd repeated the story many times over the years, of how she looked on their first date...

"Like a film star, your mother...more beautiful than Maureen O'Hara!"

They remained from the day they'd met, demonstratively, deeply in love, having married in the following Spring of 1940.

I'm probably biased but, whenever I've looked at the few 'Black & White' photographs of their Wedding Day, having since seen old films with Maureen O'Hara in the cast, can actually see the facial resemblance...even down to her slight and shapely frame, also her wonderful Auburn wavy hair. Mum and Dad, a handsome couple in every way. Feeling lucky to have been granted them as parents, and with a healthy envy of their enduring 'love'. It's so romantic the way Mum and Dad met, but I can't help being amused and thinking...

'Can you imagine a 'man' winning 'fair maiden' with an 'ice-cream' nowadays!'

Most of my other early memories are rather fuzzy but, nonetheless, they give rise to dark images of horror that are forbidding. Then, too young to understand the everyday perils we were living under in London's East End, nor what the Wartime Blitz really meant. Some of the images are vivid, but also disjointed...of being grabbed up and carried, jostled along, at a running pace, in mother's arms...the sense of danger; loud noises... terrible, indescribable smells I now recognise as the smell of death and burning flesh. These types of images are not isolated, happening on many occasions...with no recollection of how they started, or finished...of what was actually happening, at the time. To remain in the darkest corners of thought...hidden in the enclaves of my mind giving rise to nightmares of being left alone; everyone gone with me in the middle of the vast surrounding debris, as far as the eye could see! In these reoccurring nightmares, from which I would wake up screaming for many years' to follow...I knew it was our home that was the surrounding rubble, with everyone I loved dead. It also seemed as though everyone else in my whole world of understanding, was dead too? Thank God, those dreams gradually left me, as I grew older. Yet another disjointed memory, also deeply imprinted, is of being in a pushchair travelling fast along the pavement. However, this memory is obviously a 'good memory' as it's left me with a lasting love of rainfall, with its 'pitter-patter' on anything capable of making noise? I can hear the rhythmic sound of the wheels going over the cracks between the paving slabs...every so often, jolting over bumps. William, my brother is still quite small, and I'm holding him tight...it's raining very hard, making loud, frequent thuds on the canvas hood, and splashing inside from over top of the canvas covering our legs and bodies...I cannot see Mum, but I know she's there. I'm worrying that she's getting wet, yet I'm also feeling very safe in the knowledge that she's there, which makes this memory really quite a strange one to fathom? I don't recall where we'd been, but I know we are travelling along Bow Common Lane. We've come passed May's the Bakers, on the opposite side of the road, having already crossed Stink House Bridge, over the Limehouse Cut. Now, approaching the Bow Common Gas Works on the right, situated just before the arched tunnel of the railway bridge. We're going home, and I'm looking forward to getting there...once through the railway bridge, and across the alley leading to the 'barrel arches' under the railway...we'll be turning right into Cantrell Road. Only seven houses to go...I don't remember reaching the house? Perhaps, I'd fallen asleep...

Chapter Three

The War in progress...would, from its outbreak, change the face of the previously established classes, and that of the accepted role of women, uniting all, to fend off a common enemy. The women of Britain, whether Royal, aristocratic debs, women in service, factory workers, shop girls, housewives, mums or grandmothers, their courage tested beyond imagination. This was a War unlike any other before...this War, a 'Peoples' War'...hitting the very heart of the home and homeland. Whilst their able men were away fighting, the perils would continue to approach their very 'front-doors'...to steal their homes, way of life, threatening their lives and that of their children. The heart-wrenching decision was made to evacuate the children from London to country areas, to keep them safe. Hundreds and hundreds of children would sit on the Railway Station platforms, wearing cardboard labels around their necks like real-life 'Paddington Bears' some tearful, some in stunned anticipation. Their mother's looked on, 'brave faced' awaiting the moment they'd have to wave them off. Watching and waving, 'til the trains disappeared from sight, taking the children from the horrors of the Blitz. Many children were sent away, but some stayed!

Those women able to took on the work of men while others joined up into various services. Although, few women from privileged backgrounds had actively taken a role in War before...there had been some in history. The First Aid Nursing Yeomanry, which had been started during the Boar War; a group of nurses from well-to-do backgrounds, wearing red and blue uniforms, would ride out, despite the dangers, to help the wounded; but this was by no means, the norm.

However, at 11.15am on the 3rd September, 1939 Mr. Chamberlain's voice broadcast to the nation the following statement announcing that a state of war existed between Britain and Germany. The nation was in stunned silence, as he spoke these words...

"This morning the British Ambassador in Berlin handed the German Government a final Note stating that, unless we heard from them by 11 o'clock that they were prepared at once to withdraw their troops from Poland, a state of war would exist between us.

I have to tell you now that no such undertaking has been received, and that consequently this country is at war with Germany.

You can imagine what a bitter blow it is to me that all my long struggle to win peace has failed. Yet I cannot believe that there is anything more or anything different that I could have done and that would have been more successful.

Up to the very last it would have been quite possible to have arranged a peaceful and honourable settlement

between Germany and Poland, but Hitler would not
have it. He had evidently made up his mind to attack
Poland whatever happened, and although He now says
he put forward reasonable proposals which were
rejected by the Poles, that is not a true statement.
The proposals were never shown to the Poles, nor to
us, and, although they were announced in a German
broadcast on Thursday night, Hitler did not wait to
hear comments on them, but ordered his troops to
cross the Polish frontier. His action shows convincingly
that there is no chance of expecting that this man will
ever give up his practice of using force to gain his will.
He can only be stopped by force.

We and France are today, in fulfilment of our
obligations, going to the aid of Poland, who is so
bravely resisting this wicked and unprovoked attack on
her people. We have a clear conscience. We have done
all that any country could do to establish peace. The
situation in which no word given by Germany's ruler
could be trusted and no people or country could feel
themselves safe has become intolerable. And now that
we have resolved to finish it, I know that you will all
play your part with calmness and courage.

At such a moment as this the assurances of support that
we have received from the Empire are a source of
profound encouragement to us.

The Government have made plans under which it will
be possible to carry on the work of the nation in the
days of stress and strain that may be ahead. But these
plans need your help. You may be taking your part in

the fighting services or as a volunteer in one of the branches of Civil Defence. If so you will report for duty in accordance with the instructions you have received. You may be engaged in work essential to the prosecution of war for the maintenance of the life of the people - in factories, in transport, in public utility concerns, or in the supply of other necessaries of life. If so, it is of vital importance that you should carry on with your jobs.

Now may God bless you all. May He defend the right. It is the evil things that we shall be fighting against - brute force, bad faith, injustice, oppression and persecution - and against them I am certain that the right will prevail."

War...it was overwhelming...all encompassing, some people believed it was the 'end of their lives'...possibly, the 'end of the World!' The resulting levelling of the classes, in unity to fight against Hitler's tyranny, whilst heart-warming and serious...still in some strange way, appeals to my 'odd sense of humour' when visualising the reality!

Now, without hesitation, the vast majority of aristocratic girls, alongside girls of working-class back-grounds, joined-up to do their bit! For the debs, born into a world of privilege and rigid class-divide, the culture shock must have been something to behold... with doubtless comical moments of social embarrass-ment? These girls, the very top tier of society, for genera-tions brought up in a cocoon of wealth...at 18 years to be launched into smart society, and introduced into the traditional round of engagements, including a formal presentation at Buckingham Palace. Surrounded by footman, butlers, cooks and lady's maids and the like, growing up in large and lavish houses on huge estates. Their lives were of learning how to ride a horse correctly, and of acquiring the skills of etiquette of being a 'lady.' How to engage in polite conversation, hold a champagne glass, and curtsey to the King and Queen, with little else being expected of them! Alongside the woman from the working-classes, the countless upper-classes signed up to make planes and munitions in factories. Others became nurses or joined the Woman's Voluntary Service, many went on to join the Auxiliary Territory Service to man anti-aircraft batteries, and back up the Army as clerks, cooks, storekeepers, and drivers. Some of the girls were put to a wide range of transport duties, such as driving ambulances, their driving skills acquired from the family chauffeur! Within the upper-class, the more favoured services to join were the Woman's Royal Naval Service with its elegant black-blue uniform, and the previously mentioned First Aid Nursing Yeomanry, from the Boar War, now considered very 'chic'! I guess the biggest jolt for a 'lady' in this 'melting-pot' of the classes must have been, at first finding themselves sleeping next to their considered…'social inferiors'! This had the effect of being somewhat like a 'Two Ronnie's' sketch…'I look up to him'…'and I look down on him!' Becoming the 'butt-end' of endless jokes, probably cutting both ways, with a 'bitchiness' of delivery that woman can be capable of… sharp enough to be the envy of 'Wilkinson Sword!'

No matter what their background…they were all in the same boat, realising very quickly, they'd all been plunged into lives of danger, for some sexual adventure and liberation…for most experiencing first hand, life away from home and the horrors of war...sights they would never forget! Any woman, from any background, who may have once been seen as a 'delicate flower' finding herself in the thick of horrors, dealing with limbless casualties, burn victims with the indescribable smell of charred flesh, soon forgot the pettiness of class 'shaped up' and simply 'got on with it'! Their work both courageous and necessary furthermore, duly recognised as such...even by men, who had previously been just as prejudice.

Mum had originally wanted to join the Wrens, but Grandfather would have 'none of it' declaring that...

"No daughter of mine's...going to be a 'ground-sheet' for soldiers!"

But, Gran was furious with him, with the retort...

"It's good enough for the King's Daughter!"

The Blitz was tearing the heart out of London...7 Cantrell Road had, had its windows shattered and part of the roof blown off, but still it stood! Much time was spent 'going to and from' the house, the Anderson Shelter or the Tube Station along with hundreds of others, trying to avoid the bombs...now, the nights were interrupted by the frequent air raids. Previously, the Air-Raid Sirens had mostly signalled daylight raids, which became the most chilling sound imaginable at night. Its hollow warning was of 1000lb bombs, incendiaries, conjuring sinister imaginings of German parachutes dangling their 'river mines' floating silently through the night. Phosphorescent tracer bullets ripped through the night air, and the incendiary bombs popped, hurling quantities of white flame. All over London air raid shelters had been built, blackout curtains were up in every house...shops had painted their windows black.

Also, into odd scraps of earth, short posts had been hammered with flat squares of plywood, nailed to the tops. These were painted with a chemical solution, which was expected to turn green in the event of a 'gas' attack. Everyone, of every age, was issued with 'gas masks' made of black rubber, with instructions to 'carry them with you at all times, wherever you go.'

Mum, had been out during one of the first daylight raids; the siren sounded and she was transfixed to the spot. Unable to move, she found herself looking upwards to scan the sky. Something attracted her attention high up where the blue sky fades into grey... groups of silvery dots, caught by the sun. As they came nearer, she could see the shape of the wings and hear the throb of their engines. Moments later she could see hundreds of bombers, surrounded by more squadrons of Messerschmitt fighters, protecting them on their flanks. There must have been more than a 1000 planes in the air...a sight both breathtaking and terrifying. Suddenly, she felt her legs move. Mum started to run, as fast as her legs could carry her in desperation to get back home to the rest of the family...her worst fear, to be separated from everyone she loved, during a raid. Later, during the War, Hitler sent another package of terror, the V1 Flying Bomb (or doodlebug, as it was called)...it would 'drone' as it flew, when it went silent, it fell, it reduced homes to rubble, it killed. Those killed, never heard the 'one that struck!' Then the V2 Rocket Bomb followed this...it had no warning at all, a whoosh, and... devastation!

It must have been very hard to have been a parent during the War, knowing their sons may not come home; or a wife, come to that, with husbands in battle!

Mum's Brother Bill   Mum's Brother George

Every man, woman, and child at home also, instinctively aware that their lives hung in the balance, each day! Mum's two elder brothers, George and Bill had both joined-up into the Navy, whilst her older sister, Ann worked in a factory, preparing and packing medical supplies. Although George and Bill were in the Navy, they were on separate ships, and both brothers' ships, had been torpedoed and sunk, at different times and they were reported 'missing!' Many months would pass without word of their safety, for George the 'third!' time a ship he was on had been sunk. George, was still a Naval Serviceman on the previous two ships that 'went down'. Later, like my Father, he volunteered for 'Special Service' to become a Royal Naval Commando, sometimes called 'Beachhead Commandos'...taking part in the Dieppe raid in August, 1942. At Dieppe the Royal Naval Commando's suffered heavy casualties with some becoming prisoners of war. As a Royal Naval Commando,

George went through the same rigorous training as my father had to become a No. 4 Commando, although there were some differences. Not only did the Royal Naval Commandos have to go through the same training as the Army and Marine Commandos, but they also had to perform a difficult command and control task amid the chaotic conditions of an amphibious operation.

The first ship George had gone down on was called 'The Lady Somers'. The announcement came over the radio as Gran' had been cooking ...

"Today, HMS 'The Lady Somers' has been sunk in the North Atlantic by German 'U' boat torpedo..."

She'd cried out in shock..."Oh! My Georgie!"

Dropping the pan she then collapsed to the floor. This happened on the 15th July, 1941. These radio broadcasts were later stopped, as it was felt that they were a source of information to the Germans.

One of the neighbours, a lady called Mrs. Passmore, had a son who was a 'stoker' on 'The Lady Somers'...he was her only child. She would call at Gran's daily.

"Have you heard anything Mrs. Symmonds? You know, my boy can't swim. What d'ya think their chances are?"

Mrs. Passmore had known Gran' for years, she lived round the corner in Bow Common Lane...even during this time of their united 'grief' still referring to each other by title. That was the way things were done in those days...they probably never knew each other's first names!

The 'black cloud' hanging over the family began to lift, when first, word came that Bill was safe. Then some weeks on, that George had been picked up by Fishermen and taken eventually into Gibraltar, injured but alive. Mrs. Passmore came for the last time, grief-stricken...her son, Bobby was dead. A widow already...the pain of losing her only son was just too much...she died, soon after. The grief too traumatic and all-consuming to bare...

Chapter Four

During the Spring of 1940, not long after Mum &
Dad's marriage...it seemed that, not only was there
the crisis of Britain being at war with Germany, but now
a crisis brewing within Britain's Government! Who
would take over from Chamberlain? Churchill was not
the natural successor to Chamberlain as Prime Minister
in May, 1940. Lord Halifax, the Foreign Secretary, was
the preferred choice of the Conservative Party, the
King and Queen and Chamberlain himself. But Halifax
recognised that he lacked the necessary qualities to lead
Britain in war. Winston Churchill was the only possibility
once Halifax had ruled himself out.

Following the fall of France and the evacuation from
Dunkirk, Britain stood alone with the enemy occupying
most of Europe, poised to complete their conquests
with the invasion of the British Isles. With the cards
stacked against him, Winston Churchill took the bold
and imaginative step to raise a force of 'special raiding
troops' to strike back at the enemy on his newly acquired
ground.

Dad having seen a notice asking for volunteers for
'Special Service' duly applied. Although, his decision was
to the horror entwined with secret pride of Mother, who

naturally was in fear and mortal terror of losing him in battle. At the very least, she would not see him for the foreseeable future, nor would she know the nature of his secret missions. At that point neither my Mother, nor Father knew what 'Special Service' would entail?

Dad went on to become a No. 4 Commando, although still attached to his original Army Regiment...and history would tell their story, and that of many other Commando Units...of which Mum's brother George, also joined.

Taking their names from the 'mobile guerilla units' of the Boer War these units became known as 'Commandos' and wearing distinctive 'Green Berets'. Their ranks were open to all serving soldiers, volunteers came from all the different regiments and serving units in the British Army. From the beginning commando training was tough and demanding...anyone failing to attain the required high standard was returned to his unit.

Dad's Troop of comrades - Dad 3rd from right,
2nd row from top

Dad's unit, No. 4 Commando was formed in July, 1940 from some of the successful volunteers, founded by Lord Lovat.

I was less than a month old when in March, 1941 - No. 4 Commando, together with No. 3 was selected to take part in 'Operation Claymore' against the Lofoten Islands (Norwegian Territories within the Arctic Circle occupied by the Nazis).

They arrived at the Lofoten Islands in the early hours of the 4th March. The Germans were totally unaware of the attack and the troops were taken by surprise. The Fish Oil Factories and Military Installations were destroyed. One of the Commandos got into the Telegraph Office and cheekily sent a Telegram to Hitler, 'complaining about the lack of men to fight!' They then re-embarked and headed for home, returning with over 300 volunteers from the Norwegian Forces, 60 Quislings and 200 German Prisoners. Amazingly…the only casualty to be reported was an Officer who'd accidentally shot himself in the thigh!

Dad's infrequent visits home to the war-torn house of 7 Cantrell Road saw something different on each 'leave'…not knowing what he would find, became his constant worry. Originally from the corner of Cantrell Road and Bow Common Lane, the houses started with No. 1 and continued to no. 30, before the railway arch and bridge. Now houses numbered 1, 2 and 3 had gone...from no. 12 onwards up to the bridge, had also been bombed. On the opposite side of the road (opposite 7 Cantrell Road), from the corner of Bow Common Lane and up to the bridge, was the Cemetery...some of the railings were missing and graves violated by the blasts. From the railway arch and bridge just around the corner in Bow Common Lane, the railway continues to the next railway arch and bridge in Cantrell Road, along and behind our house; with the Bow Common Gas Works immediately behind the railway. This railway runs from Limehouse, near the River Thames and runs pass by at the back of 7 Cantrell Road to the next station at Bromley-by-Bow. The trains would run high up, level with the tops of the houses...and years later, when I grew older I would wave at the people in the trains, from the back top window.

When continuing on from our house, through the 'railway arch' in Cantrell Road, the road curled to become Knapp Road, which in turn meets the 'T' junction of Devons Road. All the houses, both sides of Knapp Road had been bombed, with many deaths... around 150 homes, maybe more, had been destroyed (with more bombed houses in the adjoining roads of Fairfoot Road, Spanby Road and Fern Street). Just a few houses remained in Knapp Road, near the 'T' junction on the left, and on the right of Knapp Road was the infant's entrance of Devons Road Primary School. The rest of the school, in Devons Road itself...had been battered, but still stood! One can only assume that the German Bombers' were targeting the Railway and Gas Works...they'd hit everything else but...!

In April, 1942...the birth of my brother, William... arriving on the 9th ...Mum's sister had delivered him.

Dad received the news much later by letter. In the same month of April, following the cancellation of further raids on Norwegian Territory, 'Operation Abercromby' took place. The mission involved the reconnaissance of Hardelot, Boulogne with instructions to capture prisoners and inflict as much damage as possible to the defences, including the destruction of a Searchlight Battery. The operation was delayed twice due to poor weather conditions, but the landings finally took place on the 21st - 22nd April. 100 men from No. 4 Commando and 50 men from the Canadian Carlton and York Regiment, under the overall command of Lord Lovat were selected. The operation did not go as smoothly as hoped, despite landing without opposition the troops were caught by the very Searchlight Battery they'd come to destroy; whilst still in the sand dunes had found their way hampered by wire entanglements. Caught in a hail of machine-gun fire with time running out, the attack was abandoned.

There was now a pause in the UK based Commando activity. The Dieppe raid was to be No. 4 Commando's next major assault. On the 19th August, 1942 No. 4 Commando played an important part in the ill-fated raid on Dieppe, their target being the six, 115mm guns of the Coastal Battery at Varengeville-sur-mer. There the No. 4 Commando (again under the command of Lord Lovat) carried out a 'Classic Operation'... completely destroying the guns and annihilating the Garrison. No. 4 Commando suffered 45 killed, wounded or missing from 265 Commandos. Their assault was the only success of this sad day which saw appalling casualties amongst the Canadian Troops.

Following the disaster of the Dieppe raid, and the fact that Britain was now partner to her new American Allies, the nature of the Commando's role changed. Small scale coastal raiding was given to smaller specialised units, such as the Special Operations Executive (S.O.E). The subsequent re-organisation of the S.O.E., turned them from raiders to assault infantry.

Much later, we were to learn that No. 4 Commandos' part in the Dieppe raid, code-named 'Operation Cauldron' resulted in a Training Manual being published which 7 months later was used to help train other British and Allied Soldiers. This was issued by The War Office in February, 1943 entitled 'Notes from Theatres of War - No.11 Destruction of a German Battery by No. 4 Commando During The Dieppe Raid'. The Dieppe raid also considered a rehearsal for D-Day.

Mum's brother George, now a Royal Naval Commando also took part in this raid, taking US Soldiers across on landing crafts. His 'beach party' landing the men on the beaches...some could not reach their assigned beach, due to heavy gunfire.

Despite the problems at Dieppe a lot was learnt, in particular the need for Combined Operations and within this the obvious need for Royal Naval Beach Parties, who would be vital in any major amphibious operations. It was also clear they needed specialised training and a school was established at Ardentinny, Scotland to train the RN Commandos. Meanwhile Lord Louis Mountbatten took over command of Combined Operations - motto 'United We Conquer'. Uncle George was among the first to arrive at Ardentinny along with around 500/600 men. They made good use of Loch Long for amphibious landing drills, reconnaissance and gaining specialised beach skills. Their training included weapons usage, rock climbing, assault courses, embarkation and debarkation of various types of landing craft under battle conditions, with route marches and field survival. Skills were honed at Achnacarry, where they were put through their paces by the famous Army Commando Officer, Colonel Vaughan. Uncle George passed this tough Commando training course to receive his 'Green Beret' along with the famous F-S dagger from Colonel Vaughan at a 'special parade'...it is said that their time spent at Achnacarry was responsible for the Royal Naval Commandos' new motto 'Imprimo Exulto' – 'first in last out'and worn on their RN Commando cap badge. Dad and Uncle George were to see action and later share memories of being involved in some of the same raids during the war.

May, 1943 saw Dad's unit, No. 4 Commando re-training for their new role. At Falmouth, Cornwall the Commandos took part in a cliff assault exercise "BRANDYBALL" on the 7th June. The purpose of this exercise was to prove that a force of men could be landed by the Navy on a shore, so rocky and high, that it would be undefended. The Navy considered 'that such a landing would be impossible!' But, in true style, the Commandos proved them wrong and observers from all the services, which included General Sir Bernard Montgomery, were suitably impressed.

Meanwhile Uncle George was taking part in the invasion of Sicily, Operation Husky, which involved more than 2,000 ships and landing craft. Once the assault troops were ashore the RN Commandos job was often just starting, as they usually had to work the beaches for weeks, directing in the supplies and reinforcements, guiding out the wounded and prisoners of war. As a sideline the RN Commandos took the Island of Monte Cristo which had an enemy radio station capable of plotting Allied Shipping in the area and reporting back to the mainland. They also took the Island of Pantelleria, in June, 1943

In September, 1943 George along with his unit of RN Commandos went in with the Army and Royal Marine Commandos, when the Allies landed in Italy, and later during the advance up the Italian coast helped open up anchorages. At both Salerno and Anzio, landing RN Commandos had to deal with minefields before they could signal the waiting landing craft to come in. It was treacherous work...at Anzio, George and some of his comrades had to use their F-S daggers to probe for wood encased mines which could not be located with the Royal Engineers metal detectors. Sand-bars offshore also created problems during this landing, but the RNC kept the beachhead functioning throughout the initial landings, also for months afterwards, despite constant German Shelling. As the advance moved further up the Italian Coast the RNC were given two further roles, the recovery of escaped Allied prisoners of war along the Adriatic Coastline and protecting war criminals from local inhabitants, long enough to get them back for Allied Interrogation in preparation for War Crimes Trials, once the war was over. Some of the RNC's had a break from Italy, they crossed into Yugoslavia or went down to the Greek Islands to help push to enemy back. Some Royal Naval Commandos specialised in jungle warfare at the training school at Chittagong, went on to the Far East experiencing the worst kind of warfare. George came back to England with other Royal Naval Commandos, to prepare for Normandy 'Overlord' - eight parties, mostly Canadian were scheduled and trained for this, the largest amphibious operation of the war. RN Commandos went in the first wave in order to judge whether landing craft of subsequent waves could land at the same point or go elsewhere. They took heavy casualties.

Towards 'Overlord' three Troops of No. 4 Commando were used in Manacle Operations on the Normandy Coast. Their objectives were to take out German strong-points and to conduct reconnaissance, as part of 'Layforce II'. They were unofficially known as the "Menday Force" after their Commander. No. 4 participated in Manacle 5 at Qnival and Manacle 8 at Quend Plage operating from Dover. The latter was abandoned due to rough weather. The Manacle, and associated Hardtack pin prick raids, finally abandoned on the orders of Laycock because they encouraged the enemy to reinforce their positions which could be disadvantageous to the Allies.

Within 'Overlord' - 6th June, 1944, No. 4 Commando took on an assault role. They were the first Commandos to hit the beaches on D-Day. Dad was on the 'Maid of Orleans'... (Seen here in these photographs with his comrades of D & E Troop being briefed by Lt. Col. Dawson)

Lt Col Dawson on 'Maid of Orleans' briefing D & E Troops of No. 4 Commando before D-Day (See better quality copy below courtesy of Darren Radford). This numbered copy for ease of identification. Names found on a photocopy in the collection of Ernie Brooks BEM of No.4 Commando. My father is no. 13 in the photograph L/Cpl William Oakes... 1. Jock Moore; 2. unknown; 3. Stanley Maule (kia); 4. Symes; 5.Harvey O'Hara; 6. Jimmy Linham; 7. Jenson or Jensom; 8. Lt Col. Dawson; 13. William Oakes; 15. Orlando Farnese (kia); 21. Graham Bandfield; 31. J. Fletcher; 33. Sam ...; 34. Wall; 41. Moore (medic)

In Memory of 2075115 Corporal Stanley Maule
Royal Engineers and No. 4, Commando who died age
25 on 06 June 1944 Remembered with honour at
BAYEUX WAR CEMETERY

In Memory of 7365489 Private Orlando Raffaele
Farnese Royal Army Medical Corps and No. 4,
Commando who died age 24 on 06 June 1944

500 men disembarked from their landing craft Princess
Astrid and Maid of Orleans with orders to link up with
the British 6th Airborne Division, who had dropped to
capture the bridges over the Caen Canal and the River
Orne at Benouville.

Despite casualties No. 4 Commando pushed on and
captured the town of Ouistreham before following on to
join the rest of the Brigade at the bridges, and to form a
bridgehead with the 6th Airborne Division over the River
Orne, in the area of Le Plein, Hauger/Amfreville/Breville/
Ranville.

There during the following weeks they successfully held the line, repulsing many German counter-attacks, but unfortunately casualties were high. On the 26th August they were withdrawn from the fighting having been 'continuously in action for a period of 82 days.'

Subsequently, No 4 Commando returned to England to reform, but in October was back in Europe at Den Haan, Belgium to join the 4th Special Service Brigade.

Dad came home on leave for a short period in September, 1944 before going back to continue training for what they thought would be action in the Far East, attending lectures on jungle warfare. Then receiving a sudden 'movement order' they crossed from Newhaven to Dieppe on the 6th October, to move on from there to Belgium. Arriving at Den Haan, a small place near Ostende, where Dad and his comrades moved into billets...training again, for what would be their next raid, on Flushing. Whilst he'd been home on 'leave' he'd again seen the demise of a few more local landmarks! This time the pub where he used to have a pint or two 'The Prince Albert' just around the corner in Bow Common Lane, had been bombed. People had still been singing round the piano, when the siren went off! They'd all got out safely...calling the Germans, everything imaginable! Also, bombed and reduced to rubble, further along the road from the pub...Dick di Costa's Fried Fish Shop and Mr. Thompson's Sweet Shop. Still at least Charles' Pie & Mash Shop in Burdett Road, had survived! For the moment anyway!

On the 1st November, 1944 the Brigade attacked the Island of Walcheren off the Dutch Coast, to open up the approaches to the Port of Antwerp. No. 4 Commando was given the daunting task of making a 'frontal attack' on the Port of Flushing. By 1600 hours the Commandos had reached most of its objectives, and consolidated, continuing the battle the next day.

This attack was so successful, with the Commandos capturing the greater part of the Port; it was acclaimed as a 'classic example of Commando Warfare'...No. 4 Commando was made responsible for the Walcheren Area and, after a period of rest and refitting at Ostende, spent the remainder of the War guarding the approach to Antwerp.

No.4 Commando group at Flushing, November 1944. Photo courtesy of Ann Oakes-Odger MBE, daughter of L/Cpl. William Henry Oakes No.4 Commando (Assuming 2 rows Left to right, and then one man on his own at the very front: Back / 1st row (6 men): 1-4. n/k; 4. 'Tanky' Byrne; 5. Lewis John Jones; 6. n/k 2nd row (8 men): 1. Capt. Jack 'Tug' Wilson; 2-6. n/k; 7. L/Cpl. William Oakes; 8. n/k On his own at the front on the left: Leslie Kenneth 'Ken' Fosberry. Tug Wilson was Captain of

2 troop at Flushing. Commando Veterans Association: "We have another slightly different, but better quality, version of this photo already in our gallery. Ken Fosberry, who is in the photo, states that they were on a captured ship in the dry docks at Flushing. November 1/44.Click on this link to view it: www.commandoveterans.org/ cdoGallery/v/units/4/IMG_0010.jpg.html

Again, George with the Royal Naval Commandos took part in the capture of Walcheren and in crossing the Rhine at Arnhem. It was later decided to send the RN Commandos to the Pacific to take part in the invasion of the Japanese home islands of which George and his party, along with other parties, had been picked for this task. They were joined by force X and Y from the South East Asia Command, but fortunately it was not necessary to undertake this task, once the dropping of the atomic bombs on Hiroshima and Nagasaki had brought about the a speedy conclusion to hostilities.

No. 4 Commando returned to England, having served in Germany until after VE Day...where it was officially disbanded on the lst March, 1946 having only had a strength of 180 men since June, 1945.

Chapter Five

The 8th May, 1945 was not only to mark the end of the War, but for me a new understanding of a way of life I'd never known before…it was baffling, strangely quiet… so quiet, 'it was deafening! But of course that was after the VE Day Celebrations! Before and during my short lifetime, the capital had endured 101 daylight and 253 night attacks. Which, when averaging out all the alerts, Londoners had been threatened with death, once in every 36 hours for over 5 years, astonishing! Also, to a lesser degree this applied to most of the United Kingdom. There'd been tension in the air for many days…even at my then tender age of 4 years, I'd instinctively realised 'something important was going on, something was happening'…Mum's appearance was different, more pre-occupied, tense, with an air of frustration! Gran' and Granddad too, just about everyone, we knew? Granddad had been going out early each day to get the newspaper, and constantly listening to the radio. On Wednesday 2nd May he'd come home waving the paper and shouting out…

"Hitler's dead…Hitler's dead - Doenitz appointed Fuhrer!"

Then again on Thursday 3rd May…it was still dark… we heard Grandfather, actually swearing.

"That bastard, Hitler's killed himself, the coward… he's gone and committed suicide along with Goebbels."

Plenty more was said…on a daily basis, about the situation…

"It's got to be over soon!"

He'd keep repeating. What was it all about? My brother and I could not fathom anything! Much later, as I grew older, I would wonder 'How would history, or the German peoples' view this man 'Hitler' who'd taken his nation to the brink of inhumanity, and the world to near destruction; then when faced with defeat, he'd left his people to face 'his shame' by taking his 'life!' But, then it would later transpire, that tens of thousands of Germans, also Japanese chose to kill themselves rather than begin a life under the shadow of defeat. Thousands took part in mass suicides or self-murder among the vanquished of World War II…a phenomenon almost unknown in the world since ancient times.

On the morning of Tuesday 8th May, William and I had been called to get up early, although neither of us had slept much! Granddad had already been out to buy the 'One Penny' 4am Victory Edition of the Daily Mail - for King and Empire, it's headlines

'VE-DAY - IT'S ALL OVER'.

During the previous night people seemed to be calling at the house continuously and there was lots of excited conversations going on downstairs. Unbeknown to us, shortly after we'd been put to bed at around 7.30pm, a radio announcement had been made by the Ministry of Information.

'In accordance with arrangements between the three great powers, tomorrow, Tuesday, will treated as Victory in Europe Day and will be regarded as a holiday.'

All William and I knew…there was lots of noise and fuss outside, but the noises were different! As we'd tried to sleep, tugs and motorboats on the River Thames nearby, began making long 'whooping' sounds…more boats, then more boats, joined in. I went to the window and William Kept repeating…

"What's happening? Sissy, what's happening?"

"I don't know!" I responded.

We started to call out down the stairs to Mum. She eventually came…

"Go to sleep, there's nothing to worry yourselves about."

We eventually drifted off to sleep, despite the throng, only to be awakened again around midnight! This time it was a tremendous thunderstorm, the biggest ever, the rain thrashing down, the thunder seemed louder than any bomb! Again, I ran to the window, peeping out of the smallest opening I could manage…suddenly the sky lit up like daylight by the sheets of lightning, more thunder, then jagged forks of lighting, and more thunder. Leaping back into bed, I pulled the covers over my head…gradually, after what seemed an endless time, everything slowly became quiet…

"Come on, come on, get up…rise and shine" I heard Mum saying.

Slowly, opening my eyes to see the day had dawned, beautifully clear and bright, the morning of VE Day. "Up you get"…hugging me very tight, she pulled me out of bed, and danced around the room. Then she grabbed William...dancing with both of us in her arms! She was crying, tears of joy, laughing and screaming out..."It's all over, kids...the War's over" We giggled with delight, because Mummy was so happy, but we didn't really know, what it meant?

"Does that mean Daddy will be coming home?"

"Yes, my little darlings, it does."

"What about Uncle George and Uncle Bill?"

"Yes! Yes! them too, but not today"

"When, Mummy...when?"

Just then Granny appeared and hugged us all, tears streaming down her face. "God has been kind to this family, children...we should say a prayer, everyone is safe, many families have lost everything!"...I could hear the Church bells, ringing out in the distance coming from Bow Church. Looking back on this memory, I feel sure their prayers that day were more in the hope that Dad, George and Bill would come home safe, than the actual knowledge. At that time, the last information received, Dad was still in the Walcheren Area and possibly so was George.

Bill's sporadic letters had arrived from various places during the war years such as Durban, Canada...his last known position, somewhere off the Coast of North Africa!

Mum got us dressed, going downstairs to find, everyone scurrying around relaying information from the radio, whilst Granddad was reading aloud various articles from the Daily Mail.

"Listen to this...look...here's an article written yesterday by the Daily Mail's correspondent in New York, it says here...

*"This was VE-Day in the US - official or not.
The celebrations began in New York at breakfast-time,
a few minutes after word came from France, that
Germany had surrendered unconditionally. They went
on all day despite an avalanche of confused messages,
lack of official confirmation, half denials, and a barrage
of rumours that the surrender was a hoax. The
American public, and particularly the New York public,
this time was determined that this was the end of the
War in Europe, and resolved to commemorate it. The
first reaction, and it was the same all over Manhattan,
was to jab open windows, tear up telephone directories,
and hurl paper into the streets. For hours tons upon
tons of ticker tape, torn-up newspapers, envelopes,
letters, magazines, and in some instances hats and
waste-paper baskets, cascaded down. Tens of
thousands abandoned work and rushed into the
Times-Square area, shouting and singing. Motorists
blew their hooters, factory whistles shrieked, and in
New York Bay ships sounded their sirens. Bands of
Service men and girls paraded the avenues, waving
flags, shouting and yelling. Planting kisses on strangers,
cavorting in and out of bars".*

By now Granddad was just about purple with
excitement…

"There's pictures 'ere as well…look, pictures of
celebrations last night, in Piccadilly Circus!"

He was just about to start reading more articles, when
a knock came at the front door. Granddad went to
answer the door - it was 'Tug' Wilson "C'mon out 'ere
Georgie Symmonds…the War's effing over…let's get the

show on the road!" Grandfather disappeared out the door. "Thank God for 'Tug' Wilson!" Gran' said to Mum, "I thought he'd never stop, with that newspaper!"

We followed soon after…out into the street to see the frenzied activity, cheering and shouting, hand-shaking, everyone hugging each other, people saying, "I'll bring out some tables"…then someone else's voice could be heard, proclaiming the command "You men sort out the manual stuff needed…and us women, we'll start making the food!" "That'll be Mrs. Commons no doubt!" Granny said, laughing, going on to add, "Can always rely on Ada Commons to give the orders, when order is needed!" Some years later, the whole of the 'Commons' family emigrated to Australia, on a £10 passage. They were all characters, especially Ada…sorely missed, when they left!

Soon, apparently imitating all the other little streets throughout the land, what was left of Cantrell Road had rallied together, every edible delight possible. Shops had opened for the first two hours of the day, and everyone pooled their precious hoards of dried fruit, powdered eggs, butter, flour and the women set about baking. In quick succession the tables appeared, cloths laid, soon to be laden with cakes, sandwiches, jam tarts, even lemonade...jellies and things called 'junkets!'

Chairs appeared, bonfires were built...the wood taken from the debris of the bombed houses.

Then out came the piano!

Granddad and Mr. Commons from next door, had dragged it from our 'front parlour.' All Mum's family could sing and play the piano, and Gran' especially liked to sing. Joining in after she'd finished preparing food...

Mum's young Brother John with Nan & Granddad

Uncle John, Mum's young brother was now 14 years, soon to be 15 years of age in September; also an accomplished musician, playing both the piano and accordion. He'd decided to play his accordion...standing next to the piano, whilst Granddad played. Uncle John's school sweetheart, Mary, watched him with pride.

Living close by, a street or so away...Mary had arrived with her parents, her brother and two sisters, around midday. It was an explosion of joy, the biggest party we'd ever seen! Heaven knows where all the 'stuff' came from, it was like magic...dozens of flags on string had been tied from the remaining houses across to the railings of the Cemetery, forming a 'criss-cross' over the road!

People everywhere going in and out of each other's houses, finding more items for the 'street party'...it's merrymaking and rejoicing, loud with laughter, singing and dancing! 'Landing Of Hope And Glory...

They'll Always Be An England…
Roll Out The Barrel…
Pack Up Your Troubles…
Tipperary'…the songs just kept coming!

Grandfather, sitting at the Piano, still wearing his 'cloth cap! Someone thrust a stick with a flag on, into my hand, I gave it to William; then another appeared almost immediately, we looked at each other and giggled.

We sat ourselves in the small front garden of the house, with our little flags, having already filled ourselves with too much food. Watching from behind the small wall with the metal stumps, where the railings used to be. The railings had been taken for the War effort during the early days of the war, to make guns or tanks. We watched and waited…looking intently up towards the corner of the road, expecting any minute, to see Dad appear.

He never came…we felt downhearted, but cheered up when we spotted Auntie May, turn the corner. She'd left home that morning, to go into London…it was evening now, and the 'fairy lights' around the outside the house had been switched on and some of the older children had candles in empty jam jars!

Auntie May couldn't wait to report on what she'd seen and heard, having spent some of the time during the day in Trafalgar Square, where she'd seen people jumping into the fountain and climbing up lamp-posts. Also, she'd been in Piccadilly, Regent Street, the Mall, then at Buckingham Palace "I saw the Royal Family…

…the King, he was wearing Naval Uniform…the Queen, she looked beautiful, in electric blue she was…!

Oh! Yes, and I saw the Princesses, Elizabeth and Margaret Rose…

Princess Elizabeth, well...she was wearing her ATS uniform...!" She went on...

"Then when Churchill came out onto the Balcony... well the cheers, they were just deafening, and people were shouting 'good old Winnie!'...some people even fainted and had to be carried away, over the tops of people's heads!"

Her voice getting faster..."Someone said 'he's going to make a speech'...well, I wasn't going to miss that so, I followed everyone else...it was just a sea of people... surging along 'til we stopped in Whitehall at the Ministry of Health building."

Then gasping for breath, she said. "He came out, he did...he was standing on the balcony making his 'V' sign and saying

'This is your Victory'...everyone cheered, and said back

'No! it's yours'…

…then Ernest Bevan gave three cheers for Winston and launched into 'For He's a Jolly Good Fellow'…"
Before she could blurt out anymore, Granny interrupted,

"For goodness sake May, calm down…have a drink, or something, you've gone all red in the face!"

Some of the children had metal dustbin lids…

"William shall we'd join in?"

Dashing off, through the house and out into the back yard, I found us both a dustbin lid, whilst William found two sticks; marching back through the house to the street, bashing the lids with the sticks as we went…up the street and back to catch up with the other children. They were older but welcomed us anyway, all making a terrible din…nobody seemed to mind. Then we took it in turns to use both lids, clashing them together like giant cymbals. We never knew who the other children were, they just seemed to appear, probably from another street or maybe relatives of neighbours?

"I bet we can stay up for as long as we like tonight!" I chuckled

"It's so exciting, isn't it William" laughing, as we danced in circles holding hands.

We'd never seen fireworks before, they'd been prohibited during the War, so when suddenly a rocket went up near one of the bonfires, further up the street, William and I leapt in the air with fright!

"It's okay, kids they're just fireworks…look how pretty they are!" Mum assured us…taking us to the middle of the road to point out more fireworks going up from the direction of the Thames. We were spellbound… also the searchlights were going back and forth over the sky, then pausing to form huge 'V' signs up into the night sky. We could hear all the different boats making their 'whooping' sounds, like we'd heard the night before. Uncle John was now playing the piano, and Granddad was grumbling to Mum "Why isn't your sister here yet... suppose she's off somewhere with that Freddie Thorn... did Ann tell 'you' where she was going, or when she'd be back...she wouldn't be getting away with this if your brothers were here?"

"No Dad, she didn't say...she'll be here soon, I'm sure... she's probably over Hampstead with her workmate, Joan!"

She eventually appeared, very late! Mum started whispering to Auntie Ann or Cissy as everyone called her...

"Dad's been complaining that you weren't here...it's nearly midnight, he'll go mad...I told him you were probably with Joan!" Aunt Cis' replied, with a high pitched tone of innocence! "I was...and you'll never guess what they did to that 'dummy town' I told you about...they..."

"C'mon Ann, we're not silly...if you've been with Fred, you'd better own up!" Mum protested. "Where is he now, surely he brought you home?"

"He's round the corner, waiting with Joan and her chap, Sid!" Granddad spotted Mum, talking to Ann, and stormed over...

"Before you say anything Ann, I know Fred's hiding round the corner, I've just seen him...go and get him, and let's get the formalities 'out of the way'...I'm fed up with this nonsense...and, you can think yourself lucky 'my girl!'

Ann went to fetch Fred, along with Joan and Sid. They all shook hands..."Thank you Mr. Symmonds...

Aunt Ann (Aunt Cis'...)

I didn't mean to keep Ann out so late...I'm extremely sorry, Mr. Symmonds!" Fred was saying, going on to tell him about the 'goings on' at Hampstead Heath. We crept closer to listen, as Mum, Gran and Granddad, joined also by Auntie May, sat down with Aunt Ann (Cissy), her mate Joan and Sid...as Fred, who became very animated as he began to tell all...

"We didn't know what it was all about when we first started work, Mr. Symmonds...we were sent to Hampstead Heath with plans and specifications for this dummy town? Once work was well under way, we were told that the town was being built to confuse the Luftwaffe!"

His voice now became a very secretive whisper, as though people shouldn't hear, with a sort of MI5 air of secrecy.

"Well...I, well you see...I wanted Ann to see it Mr. Symmonds...when we got there...'er...well...'it was just starting to go up in flames!'

People had even made life-sized effigies of Adolf Hitler.... it was the most amazing sight...we just forgot the time!. Then...'er...Joan started taking pictures with her 'Box Brownie Camera!"

Grandfather coughed and interrupted...

"All very interesting Fred...very interesting...let's all get a drink, and join in the party!" Granddad made his way back to the piano...grinning all the way, and muttering "So this is my Daughter's...George Raft?"

They married soon after when he officially became 'Uncle Fred'...he and Aunt Cis' were very happy.

At midnight...everyone had made sure they'd got a drink waiting for the 'one minute past' to denote the official time of the end of the war in Europe, and up went the cheers again!

As soon as Big Ben sounded so, there was more dancing...

'Knees Up Mother Brown' followed by the 'Conga'... the snake-like stream of people, getting longer and longer!

We marvelled at everything especially the sight of street lights...we'd never before seen the 'glow' of street lights! There had only ever been one street lamp in the whole of Cantrell Road, outside No. 9 that had survived and was working! Someone had tied a rope from the metal arm protruding from the side of the lamp post, which was up near the light itself, and the older kids were swinging on it.

Gradually, people drifted away until a nucleus was left, made up of the remaining residents of Cantrell Road and their immediate families. William had fallen asleep, and it was only the sheer nosiness of 'not wanting to miss anything' that kept jolting my eyes open, whenever they started to close. Everyone had already congregated outside our house, where more serious issues were now being discussed such as, what everyone would do now? Grandfather seemed to be becoming the unofficial 'spokesperson' with residents looking to him for guidance.

"Well, we need to pull together...first things first... I think us men could probably pull resources to get each other's houses sorted...starting with 'Tug's...his house has the most damage!

Let's all agree that the men of each house have a meeting tomorrow, here at No. 7, at say...10am. The woman can stay at home to take care of the domestic end of things, while we thrash out a plan!" They were all more than agreeable, shaking hands, thanking Granddad, over and over.

Chapter Six

Mum and Granny had prepared the front parlour, and as 10am approached so the neighbours began to arrive. 'Tug' was the first, as he'd been staying at his sister's with his wife and children, a few streets away in Southern Grove. Out of the original 30 houses in Cantrell Road, from the corner to the railway bridge, only 8 remained having sustained various degrees of bomb damage. Grandfather was in fact, the street's most senior member, a second generation tenant, who'd been born in No. 7, grew up and remained there after his parents died.

Grandfather had fought in the First World War 1914/18 strangely called the Great War and experienced the hardships of the 'Depression'.

Grandfather had descended from a long line of dock workers since the 1800's and broken away from family tradition to become a master builder. His building skills were to prove invaluable to his neighbours, who were heavily reliant upon his knowledge.

Although he'd come out of the docks at an early age, the attachment to his past was still evident.

The 'Symmonds' family, Port of London 'talisman' was kept hanging in a glass case on the wall of Gran' and Grandad's bedroom. It was made of leather, into which there were lots of uniformed punch holes, at the bottom of the leather section was attached a shaped brass plate, engraved with 'Wm. Symmonds Fellowship Porter 11th February, 1829 No. I H 4'.

Mr. Middlebrook lived at No. 4 Cantrell Road with his wife May; their Son was a Merchant Seaman, and still away from home. Mr. Middlebrook had worked as a Civil Servant.

Next at No. 5 was Mr. Hayward a former publican; his wife had died just before the war leaving three sons, all of which were in the forces.

Mr. Keale lived next door to us in No. 6 with his wife Mary and Joyce, their daughter. He'd worked on the railways.

Then next door to us again, at No. 8 was Mr. Commons, an army cook, who'd arrived home quite recently, after sustaining injuries. He and his wife Ada had two young children, a boy and a girl.

At No. 9 lived Mr. Luck, Mrs. Luck and their teenage daughter, Vivien. Mr. Luck worked in the Bow Common Gas Works, at the back, behind the railway.

Mr. and Mrs. Towler with their daughter Janet, lived at No. 10, he too was a railwayman. Then the last of the surviving houses, No. 11 which belonged to 'Tug' Wilson. Tug and Mrs. Wilson's two sons were still away at sea, in the Navy.

The men from each household had all now arrived and were seated in the front parlour. A tea tray was set, which Gran' took through to them.

Mum and Gran spent much time that day, talking about the situation in the Far East, as did the men in the front parlour. There was a great deal of concern, now the previous day's celebrations had given way to reality. The war still continued in the Far East…would Dad be sent there to fight?

Would Uncle George and Uncle Bill be sent to carrying on fighting?

Our neighbours, who had relatives in the forces and still away from home, also had these worries. Many soldiers already home had taken part in the celebrations the day before, but not ours…and many men would never come home at all. Gran' said to Mum, over and over "Please God, bring our boys home soon!"

There were fears and rumours that the Japanese war could continue in the Pacific for another two years. During the months following VE-Day, the world would witness the horror of the A-bomb, and much hardship on the home front.

The men of the street had been talking for hours..... teas had gone in, sandwiches too. William and I played in the back-yard while Mum and Gran started taking tape off the windows, cleaning them, putting up lovely flowered curtains and folding away the 'black-out' blinds. Auntie May (Grandfather's sister) had gone off to work early in the morning, also Mum's sister, Ann. Our house was looking beautiful.

Although, from the outside the house looked like a 'two up, two down' terrace, it was actually very big.

From the front, there was a large 'bay window' top and bottom of the building, with white cement cornice around. Looking at the house, the front door was at the right side of the downstairs 'bay window' with an impressive arched porch.

This porch had white moulded cement embellishment on each side, up and around the arch to meet the 'keystone' at the centre top. In the middle of the 'keystone' was a moulded paterae.

Immediately above the front door on the upper floor, was another large window with the same theme of white cement embellishment, arched also to compliment the porch. When entering the house the front parlour was to the left, this room was of course the best room of the house, used for special occasions and still had very grand 'gas lights'...opening the door to this room was a feast of grandeur.

Although 7 Cantrell Road had electricity, it was a limited supply called 'Fixed Price Electricity'...basically you'd paid to have 'a light fitted' one or more; then when the 'light bulb' stopped working it was taken to the

'Electric Office' to get an exchange bulb and to pay for the electricity on a special book...there was no 'popping off' to the local shop to buy a new light-bulb! Once when it had been raining heavily the electric wires had become 'live' it made the whole house 'electrified'...even the bar of soap in the scullery was 'live!' Granny had screamed out after picking up the soap and getting an 'electric shock'...launching the soap into the air!

Entering the front parlour to the left, always stood the piano then at the bay window hung 'lined' rich green velvet curtains with gathered 'swags and drops' around the top, edged with hanging gold braid, in the window stood a jardinière with an a Aspidistra plant. Moving round the room came the Mantelpiece made of beautifully polished 'Oak' intricately carved, standing high and dominant with Corinthian columns each side and ionic capitals, supporting shelves.

Then about 6 inches above the shelves was the mantelshelf itself, from which hung swags and drops of green velvet with gold braid, matching the window curtains.

Sitting on the mantelshelf was the over-mantel that went almost to the ceiling, again made of oak, with mirror-backed carved shelves each side of the large mirror. An enormous marble clock sat on this mantelpiece, which was a complete replica of the front view of St. Paul's Cathedral, alongside were many ornaments.

Beautiful marble surrounded the fireplace opening and a marble hearth, around it a leather topped fender, you could sit on.

The fire-grate itself, was black cast iron with brass finials, which Gran' always kept highly polished and a fire was always prepared, ready to light.

In the alcoves at each side of the mantelpiece were the 'gas wall lights' with beautiful crystal drops. There was a matching crystal chandelier hanging from the centre of the ornate plaster ceiling rose. The original cornice had an 'egg and dart' motive on which followed around the ceiling line and into the bay windows. Thankfully, everything had survived the bombing, the lavish furniture too, which was made of highly polished rich dark wood, inlaid with patterns made of light wood on the table and chairs. There was a sofa with several armchairs and plump feather cushions.

Double, dark wood doors opened out from this room into the back parlour, containing another mantelpiece and over-mantel, with more crystal gas lights. Two exquisite vases with crystal lustre drops, stood one each end of the mantelshelf.

At the far end, was a large window overlooking the side walkway to the back of the house, again with green velvet curtains, in front of which stood a dark wood writing desk. Other pieces of excellent Edwardian style furniture stood in this room, consisting of cabinets, little tables, and a leather chaise. This room had its own door leading back into the hall, near the stairs to the upper floor.

Walking along the hall towards the back of the house, with the stairs on the right, was a step down into another small hallway and a door out to the side walkway leading to the yard. To the right was a door, under the stairs which led down to the cellar, and immediately in front, was the door leading the kitchenette. When entering the kitchenette there was another table and chairs, near the window to the left, and to the right was the kitchen range, which Gran' always kept in 'tip-top' condition. It was black cast iron, with all the steel parts kept gleaming, through constant polishing with 'steel wool'.

It was set back in a deep alcove, from the top of which pots hung on large hooks; a full kettle was always simmering over the fire. The fire opening at the front had vertical bars, with the fire inside filling the whole cavity in one glowing red mass; we would put slices of bread on a big fork and hold it in front of these bars to make delicious toast, tasting mildly of the glowing embers. The oven and other hotplates also produced food with its own distinctive flavour...anything cooked on the 'range' was simply fantastic, especially the bread.

Walking towards the back of the kitchenette was yet another doorway, through which stepped down into the scullery and from there, a door leading to the back-yard.

In the scullery was the butler sink in the corner, attached to which was a bleached wood draining board, with deep grooves.

Next to the window over-looking the yard, a gas cooker sat in the opposite corner from the sink. At the side of the cooker stood a wooden cabinet with an enamel top, serving as a worktop. Plates, cups and saucers, and other crockery could be stored in this cabinet, also knives and forks in the drawers.

Pots and pans hung from ceiling hooks, with a wooden airing line, made up of four or five wooden slats, secured with a pulley to the wall. Another alcove in the scullery housed a deep metal tub with a tap at the bottom to empty it, with a fire grate underneath. A curtain hung at the alcove opening, tied back to the wall. The large mangle which was set on wheels and kept in the scullery was often taken into the yard during the summer to do the washing outside to be hung straight on the line.

The toilet was outside and had no light, so when it was dark it was a terrifying experience, imagining all sorts of horrifying creatures lurking there, waiting to pounce! In the winter Grandfather would put his coat, scarf and cap on, just to venture out there, taking the newspaper. I always found very funny, as who would really want to be out in the cold, long enough to read the paper?

As a 'small person' this appeared to be one of life's mysteries...of which there were many? Oh! I would ponder, how would I ever know, all the things 'grown ups' know?

Upstairs, there was five bedrooms and on the landing another door which took you up into the attic.

Grandad had made this attic into two large rooms with one small window in each, up in the apex of the roof.

The back attic room was my favourite room, as I could see the people in the trains, from the small attic window.

William and I were later allowed to have an attic room each, and I was over the moon to get the room at the back, where I could see the trains whenever I wanted. There was never any doubt when a train was approaching or chance of missing it, as you could hear the train whistle out and the steam could be seen billowing up from the engine. A sort of rumble was felt through the whole house, not that it was strong enough to knock anything down, but it was there and it became very loud as it passed by.

I would wonder constantly 'about the people on the trains' were they rich and important, where were they going, where had they been, and what did they do?' And I made the promise to myself 'to travel on that train one day!' Which I did eventually do to my delight...

Out in the back yard was the 'Anderson Shelter' which took up quite a big area, with weeds, grass and some flowers growing on the top, and Grandfather's shed standing nearby.

There were rabbits in the yard, one was called 'Big Bertha' on account of her large size...she was a 'Flemish Giant!' He also kept chickens which gave us fresh eggs when most people had to suffer dried eggs!

The rabbits and chicken were bred for the table but, I never could work out what rabbit was coupled with 'Big Bertha' and never dared ask...another of life's mysteries!

On the fence between our back yard and next door's where the 'Commons' family lived, hung a wooden cabinet with two doors called the 'safe!' Inside the frame of the doors to the safe, was very fine wire meshing, which allowed the air to circulate and stop the 'creepy-crawlies' getting in to eat the food. The 'safe' was where things like butter, cheese and meat were kept cool on a slab of marble (not that we'd seen much of any of those luxuries due to the rationing).

I'll never really understand why we had this 'safe' at all, but everyone seemed to have them! In the summer... how could it keep food cool?

What was the difference whether the 'safe' was inside, or out?

As a child, a 'small person' this seemed to be another one of 'life's mysteries?'

Despite the other surviving houses being the same design, I came to realise that No. 7 was in, East End terms and standards, considered by our neighbours to be very 'posh' indeed, no doubt because of all the lovely décor and furniture.

Apparently, the Naval ancestors had the opportunity of acquiring fine pieces of furniture, china ornaments and the like which Grandfather had inherited; these were his and Gran's 'pride and joy!'

Regardless of what financial hardships they'd experienced, these treasured items were kept, never to be sold.

In those days, there was little or no financial help; if a person fell on hard times they simply had to sell anything of value to get by. Nan and Granddad ran a 'tight ship' the home was their castle and they had always managed to put food on the table, and keep the home together. Grandfather was a great provider and Gran' a thrifty wife.

Some of the 'Symmonds' family distant relatives were very wealthy one was Aunt Rose who lived in a big house in Chigwell. She came to see us once...she spoke with a 'polished' accent! I took note, deciding that this was how 'rich people spoke!' Trying to mimic her...made everyone laugh but, I was being quite serious!

We also had relatives in Ireland, Australia, Canada and America, said to be 'well-off!' The 'Symmonds' family, they are everywhere I mussed.

There were always lots of photographs around the house; we'd probably never get to meet most of them!

There were houses in some of the surrounding slum areas of the East End, where people did live in bad conditions. Before the war Grandfather worked in some of the houses near the Docks, where he'd seen rats, cockroaches...bed bugs, and even had to burn off wallpaper with a blow-torch which had beetles crawling between the paper and the distempered walls.

But, thankfully, we'd never experienced this in our house, nor did any of our family, friends or neighbours. In fact, during the whole of my childhood I only ever saw people who took great pride in keeping their homes clean.

Although we never had a bathroom, we were always kept spotlessly clean with clean clothes. We were always taught good table manners, rarely hearing bad language… and, never dared to get up to the table to eat without first washing our hands!

Every morning the front step was whitened and God help anyone who put a footprint on it!

Once Grandfather had 'organised' the street's workforce and the remedial work got underway, our street of only eight houses, became the envy of many surrounding streets. Many other streets formed work coalitions, as it was the only way to try and re-build what little they had left.

But, rebuilding work was very hard to achieve without the knowledge and materials…shortages of cement, bricks, steel, coal, food and clothing persisted for years after the end of the war.

Many homes were far too damaged to ever re-build and those families were left homeless.

Chapter Seven

Auntie May, arrived home from work...Granny had prepared a lamb stew with suet dumplings earlier that day which had been slowly cooking on the coal fired kitchenette range, it was nearly time to eat so William and I were sent off to wash. I could hardly wait as this was my very favourite meal. I also liked Gran's pork and rabbit stew. Another meal I adored was savoury suet roll. Mum or Granny would make it by laying the suet mix in a long flat oblong and putting pieces of bacon, sage and onion all the way along, then it would be rolled, wrapped in muslin cloth which was tied at each end and boiled; it was beautiful especially with Pease pudding.

Although meat was rationed, like many other things, a healthy trade in 'black market' products made it possible to get some luxuries, if you knew the right people and of course, for the right price!

Though we'd been sent to wash and get ready to eat, today we would have to wait longer than usual as the 'eight man delegation' were still finalising their building plans.

They'd been up and down the road surveying the situation, quantifying materials and were currently discussing the rebuilding of Tug's house.

Eventually, Grandfather appeared...we all finally sat and ate, whilst being informed of the 'plan of action' for the following day's work.

Grandfather announced that he would be up and out before 8am, meeting with the other men, down at No. 1l Cantrell Road, to get started.

Work started in earnest the next morning, by first forming a chain of men, finding the best bricks, passing them along the chain to stack. Even the women and older children joined in, but William and I grovelled around in the rubble looking for beetles, we had great fun and simply got dirty!

They also sorted out floor boards, roof timbers, roof tiles, doors and window frames, anything of any possible use, was kept. Everyone, at different times, saying to Granddad, 'George Symmonds, are you sure Tug's house can be saved...it looks pretty bad?'

Tug himself was virtually pleading with Grandfather.

The damage was certainly bad! Part of the adjoining wall to what was No. 12, had been left with a vast hole in the upper floor with floor boards hanging down to the ground floor at the rear of the house, and around two thirds of the roof was off!

There was even a bed dangling precariously from the hole, the metal bed frame twisted and buckled.

As the weeks passed, the house took shape, but it was difficult to get some of the materials, such as cement. There was no doubting it was a huge undertaking.

Granny said to Mum several times "I can't believe your Father's doing this...he's no 'spring chicken' and him and 'Tug'...well, they never even saw 'eye to eye' all the years he's lived here?"

"Yes, but don't you think...Mum, it's become Dad's personal challenge...and at least he's not moaning about the rationing and the Government!" Mum reasoned...

"True!" Gran' agreed.

May turned to June, and then July came and went!

There was public apathy and discontent as rationing was as bad as ever, with more of the same 'make do, and mend!'

There was deep grief among those that had lost their 'loved-ones'...with those men who'd already arrived home from War, finding it hard to adjust to 'civvy' life!

They'd simply forgotten what life out of a uniform was like!

Worse still, for those who'd returned home to find their whole families dead, or wives who had betrayed them with other men.

Babies born to women by men other than their husband were outcast and they were extremely lucky if their husbands were forgiving enough to take on the child as their own.

Some men even experienced a 'secret sickness of the mind' that was never be spoken of, or cured; for them there was no sophisticated counselling or understanding of 'Post Traumatic Stress Syndrome'.

Whether soldier or civilian, man, woman, or child the benefit of 'mental healing' from the horrors witnessed during those years' just didn't exist, especially on such a scale. The mental health care that did exist was still in the dark ages and asylums, feared places!

For some of the older children other difficulties emerged, Mummy had been their protector, all they'd known; the man that came home was their Daddy, but he was still a 'stranger!'

Boys and girls evacuated to the country or sent abroad to Canada or America came home to surroundings and parents they hadn't seen for years. Although, some of the lucky children who'd stayed in London, survived the blitz, and fortunate enough never to experience death of a relative or see mutilated bodies, found the war years quite thrilling!

Granny was particularly tearful one morning, having heard that Uncle George was being sent to the Far East to fight...she was beside herself.

But, as July turned to August the first A-bomb was dropped on the 6th day and the world would never be allowed forget the recorded sights of the great 'mushroom of devastation' of Hiroshima and Nagasaki.

Although the Allied nations were relieved that they been spared a bloody invasion of Japan; the arrival of the Atomic Age was an awesome and appalling 'spectre' of destructive power.

The Japanese surrendered on the 10th August, 1945, with the Emperor of Japan acknowledging surrender on the 14th August.

By the war's end the relations between the three principal members of the Grand Alliance, the United States, Russia and Britain were strained to near breaking point. Atrocities were still being committed by Soviet troops, who were killing Poles, Czechs, Hungarians and any other East European who resisted Communist tyranny.

Britain had declared war on Germany on 3rd September, 1939, when the Nazis invaded Poland. In 1945, the Poles, like millions of other East Europeans found themselves victims of Stalin's tyranny.

His tyranny was at least as brutal as that of Hitler!

Even as crowds again thronged the streets in celebration of VJ-Day, the economist John Maynard Keynes warned the British Government that it faced 'a financial Dunkirk'.

The United States emerged from World War II richer than ever, by contrast, Britain paid for its principled resistance to Nazism since 1939 with destitution.

Churchill's private secretary, Jock Colville wrote with some foresight, just before the end of the war:

'Sadly, I reflect how much easier it will be to forgive our present enemies in their future misery, starvation and weakness than to reconcile ourselves to the past claims and future demands of our two great Allies. The Americans have become very unpopular in England.'

The General Election in July, 1945 saw a surprise landslide victory for the Labour Party and Clement Attlee became Prime Minister.

Attlee came from a very privileged background, his father was a Lawyer. At aged 13 years he was sent to one of the best public schools, later to graduate from Oxford. But, it was during his work as a volunteer charity worker that he first became aware of the poverty in London's East End, and genuinely wanted to improve conditions.

He was a very different character from that of Churchill, who would be chauffeured around in limousines.

Attlee preferred to be driven by his wife in their Hillman Minx.

On one occasion arriving at the Palace, his wife sat outside in the Hillman to wait, but Palace officials upon realising it was Attlee's wife came and took her inside.

He was responsible for the birth of the National Health Service, the Welfare State and Nationalisation, but within one month of becoming Prime Minister he was to face further huge problems in the economy.

America, at the end of the war cancelled the 'Lend-Lease Agreement'.

From 1918 the U.S. had become the supreme financial power and the U.K. was faced with the fact that 'it' was 'no longer a great power, with an Empire!' Despite three months of negotiations with the U.S. asking for a grant; on the 6th December, 1945 the Anglo American Loan Agreement was signed. This was an interest bearing loan, part of the agreement to include the replacement of Sterling, as the International trading currency, for the Dollar.

Convertibility would come into effect the following year, which then devalued the pound. This agreement changed the whole course of the British economy, resulting in prolonged hardships and rationing.

German prisoners of war were kept here in their thousands, eventually totalling 385,000 with many being sent to work on farms, after being graded according to their degree of considered Nazi attitudes 'white, grey or black'.

The colour black being the grade for the highest degree of Nazism and put through a process of de-nazification.

Attlee was against repatriation of the Germans POW's allowing only 3,000 per month to go home, then 15,000 per month 'til finally the last was allowed to leave in 1948, but some 24,000 Germans decided to stay here in Britain.

I'd wondered many times, what a German looked like, and asked Mummy one day. Mum and Granny were out in the yard doing the washing…Mum was scrubbing the shirts against the washboard with a big square bar of soap, and Granny was rinsing and putting them through the mangle to hang on the line.

"Mummy, what does a German look like, how would we know if one was coming in the house?"

I'm not sure whether I'd expected Mum to tell me that Germans had 'demonic horns' and glowed in the dark, but I felt disappointed and cheated to hear her describe them as rather ordinary!

Granny was laughing whilst saying to Mum…

"Do you remember hearing about the German that bailed out of his plane and parachuted down into one of the back yards, a few streets away…?"

William and I immediately interrupted, jumping up and down with impatience

"What happened then Granny…Oh! Tell us what looked like?"

Granny responded with animated exuberance…!

"Apparently, the two women in the house rushed out, poking and hitting the German invader with brooms, until they finally uncovered him and saw he was just a young man who looked very frightened! They got him a chair, sat him down and made him a cup of tea!"

"What happened then, Gran…what did they do with him?"

Granny said, still laughing with Mum

"Well…they went and got their other neighbours who looked him over. They were trying to talk to him by waving their hands about in a sort of sign language, when suddenly he spoke to them in perfect English! He was very apologetic and thanked them for the tea…then eventually he was taken away by the Police I suppose!"

We giggled...finally we went off to play, making 'mud pies'.

It had been a long hard day for Mum and Gran, as they'd been bringing down the feather mattresses, bolsters and pillows from the beds, hanging them over the line to air and banging out the dust, as well as doing the week's washing.

Having received word that Dad, Uncle Bill and Uncle George were safe and would be coming home in the not too distant future, Gran' wanted everything cleaned and ready for them, especially while the weather held.

Each day we would help water the vegetables, every possible piece of earth capable of growing food having been planted with potatoes, runner beans, spinach and other vegetables, even in pots, barrels and old dustbins! Each night when Granddad arrived home he'd bring oddments of wood to stack in the garden, as it was unlikely there would be coal for the winter due to the continued shortages.

September turned to October without word of when Dad would be home, but Mum kept busy by making us some new clothes out of some remnants of material. She made William a complete 'sailor suit' every detail a perfect replica of naval dress but, he had to wait for Christmas before he was allowed to wear it and even then it had room for growth!

I also had to wait to wear my new outfit.

I couldn't wait for Christmas to wear these new clothes as most of my clothes were 'hand-me-downs' which included the much hated 'liberty bodices!' These bodices were restrictive and tight fitting with boned sections, which buttoned through with little cotton buttons.

I would try to avoid putting it on when getting dressed and try and hide it but, Mum always caught me. She would then 'wag her finger' reminding me of how lucky I should consider myself to have such lovely under garments!

I was never convinced!

It was a cold and crisp, frosty morning that threatened snow at the end of November when 'Tugs' house was finally completed! He'd managed to get hold of a large wooden cart which pivoted on two large metal edged wheels which he used to start moving his family back home.

Everything they owned went on it in only one trip, as virtually all they'd previously possessed had been either damaged or destroyed when the bomb hit.

As he trundled off, the cart's metal rimmed wheels made a hell of a racket over the cobbled road, whilst everyone else from the street went along to No. 11, hiding inside to surprise and welcome them back. Each household took something they could spare to help make their house more homely, also a little food and drink to have a celebration. Again, a celebration would break the gloom of 'going without' by having a party and a 'knees-up'...it was great!'

In fact, the party was also to celebrate every one of the eight houses being repaired, as over the months, whenever work had stopped at No. 11 due to shortages of materials, they would press on with a job on someone else's house.

The rest of the street and many surrounding streets still lay in ruins, and would remain so for a long time to come! But, the bond that had been forged between our family and the other seven families was now so tight that help was always there if anyone was in trouble. Everyone looked out for each other and their children with Grandfather becoming, especially in as far as 'Tug' was concerned the 'hero of the day!'

They'd become and would remain the closest of friends.

It was a good time for everyone now the houses were sound, as our little community could now solely concentrate during December in making preparation for the first peacetime Christmas.

"Christmas puddings would have to be rushed!" Granny exclaimed.

She liked to start making them in October, although they weren't made at all during the war years, so William and I had never tasted them before!

Preparation started with two large porcelain bowls being brought down from upstairs! They normally stood on the 'marble topped' washstands.

Mum started making Christmas puddings in one, whilst Granny made more in the other. They would have to make do this year with whatever ingredients they could get, but Granny insisted and declared...

"These puddings have got to have Stout in them, at the very least! 'Pops' will just have to call in a favour...I'll not put up with something tasting like 'bread pudding' for Christmas...not this year!"

Mum laughed!

The many 'cloth topped' basins were put in saucepans of water, either on the kitchenette range or out in the scullery on the gas cooker to boil.

The radio would be on all day in the background, whilst household chores and cooking was done, and William and I would play with our little wooden toys.

We'd gallop around with a broom each, pretending to ride horses...

So, Granddad decided to make us each a wooden one, which consisted of a shaped horse's head on a pole with string from its mouth.

In the evening we'd all listen to a story on the radio or play a game before bed, but if Glenn Miller music came on, the volume was turned up and Mum and Granny would start dancing around the kitchenette, then we'd all join in.

One day, when I'd remembered what one of the children had said at the VE Day celebrations, I said to Mum...

"It's good we still have stuff on the radio, isn't it Mummy, and we still get the news?" "Why wouldn't we?" Mum replied.

"Well, don't you remember, Mummy that Johnny said to his Mummy...that now the War's over, they'd be no more news?"

Mum laughed, saying...

"That's really clever of Johnny...after 5 years of hearing only news about the War...it must have seemed to him as though there would be 'no more news' left to tell! But, they'll always be news...everyday!" She assured me.

Granddad usually left the house early going off now with 'Tug' on his boat, and although I never really knew what they did all day, he'd always return home with something, money, food or wood. They would either work on the boat or on building repairs together for other people, sometimes even arriving home 'worse for wear' after a 'jar too many of beer!' Although not often, on those occasions he'd come home 'tipsy' he'd start playing the piano...and, when Gran's annoyance gave way to her smiling, he'd wink at us and give us a 'farthing!'

Each week the household money was 'pooled' Auntie May, and Granddad would give the money to Granny. Gran' would then work out how much was needed for the Rent, food and other bills, then whatever was left, would be shared out.

The front and back parlour rooms were decorated and ready for Christmas. We'd made holly wreaths and put one on the outside of the front door and collected berries, flowers also twigs from gardens of the uninhabited bombed houses. For weeks we'd made paper decorations out of bits of newspaper or magazines and everything was looking lovely...we were so excited.

It was Christmas Eve...

"C'mon William, let's go and have a look at the decorations!"

Some of the neighbours had congregated in the kitchenette, we wouldn't be missed so, we crept into the front parlour and sat down near the hearth.

"This must be the chimney that Father Christmas will come down...it's far too small for him to fit down the one in the kitchenette...anyway, the fire's always alight there, too!" William scoffed in disgust!...

"He's never come down it before!"

"Well, William, that's because he couldn't come 'down it' before, because of the bombs and...well, the Reindeers wouldn't have been able to come would they, with all those planes...Reindeers are too shy!"

Suddenly, William announced!

"I'm going to be 4 years old soon...and I don't think I want to be William anymore...I want to be Bill, like Daddy!"

"Well, you can't be Bill...only grown up men can be Bill...but, you can be Billy if you want?

Anyway...I'll be 5 years and starting school, before you're 4 years!" I replied, folding my arms, gesturing with a sort of Shirley Temple 'snotty' air of superiority.

"I'm telling Mummy of you...you're being nasty to me!"

William was about to spill the beans, I knew I would be in trouble, at the very least for going in the front room, when told not to.

"But!" he went on, "if you call be 'Billy' from now on...'til I'm big enough to be 'Bill'...I'll not tell...you'll have to promise!"

"Okay! Billy it is...I promise, and I'm sorry I was horrid!

Quick! We'd better scoot, before we get caught!"

Mum got us ready for bed, and my hair was tied in rags, so that I'd have perfect 'ringlets' for Christmas Day...we'd also be wearing our new clothes...it couldn't be morning quick enough!

Chapter Eight

We awoke on Christmas Day bright and early, despite our lack of sleep due to over-excitement!

"Billy, Billy...quick...he's been...Father Christmas, he's left us presents!"

Rushing to see what was in the stockings Mummy had made, hanging at the end of the bed. We both tipped the contents out to find, we each had an apple and a little box, wrapped in colourful paper. Ripping off the paper, I discovered a pretty miniature dolly, perfectly dressed in tiny clothes, complete with a cloak and bonnet...she was delightful. It was in fact a little dolly peg doll, that Mum had made.

"What's in your box...Billy?"

"Wow...it's an aeroplane...look!"

Just then Mum came in...

"Happy Christmas, kids"...giving us a big hug, also telling us that we're to receive another special gift later if we're good!

"Is it Daddy, is he coming home today?"

"Sadly children, we'll have to wait a bit longer to see Daddy!"

Mum decided I would be first to get ready, sitting me on the damp wooden draining board in the scullery, it's ridges still warm from the washing up! I sat swinging my legs over the edge, impatiently waiting to have my hands and face washed. We had to hurry as Mrs. Commons would be calling to take us at 10am to collect our special gifts?

Billy couldn't wait and got himself dressed, his clothes looking all lopsided. I was complaining about my hair still being in the rags! I was told in no uncertain terms that I would be wearing a hat and would not have the rags taken out 'til later that day…if I wasn't careful, I would not be going at all…nor, would not I get a present!

I soon 'shut-up!'

There was about six of us in all, and Mrs. Commons rounded us up with military precision, and when she 'boomed' out a command, we all snapped to it! Janet Towler from No. 10 was a similar age to me, so we started to make friends whilst being ushered along the road, deciding that when we started school in the New Year we would sit together.

We were marched up Cantrell Road, through the arch of the railway, into Knapp Road and on into Fairfoot Road 'til we reached almost the end of the road. It seemed a long way, but we arrived to see lots of other children queuing outside one of the few houses that hadn't been bombed. It was all very curious and thrilling.

As we got closer, I could see a 'wooden archway' that each child stepped through, and on the other side there was a lady sitting at a table taking the children's names, giving them a little bundle wrapped in newspaper and tied up with string. I was getting more and more excited, so much so, that I started to feel quite sick, light-headed and feeling as though I would burst!

"Quick, please be quick...if they don't get to us soon, Janet, I'll faint, ruin everything and look really silly!" I squawked.

Thankfully it was now my turn, Billy had already gone through the arch and was waiting at the end of the table, fidgeting with the bundle he'd been given.

I reached him just as he'd managed to break the string, spilling all the contents over the pavement, for a moment I just looked as the sweets rolled about the ground. Then rushing to pick everything up, before they were lost whilst inspecting the goodies... "Look Billy, pencils, a drawing book, sweets and paper hats...wow!"

Someone found a paper bag for Billy's presents and Mrs. Commons gave us 'the quick march' to make for home. On the way back, Billy started to sing...

He was getting louder and louder 'til eventually everyone started to join in...

"Maybe it's because I'm a Londoner, that I Love London Town..."

Each time the song stopped, so Billy would start again, with a chorus from the rest of us. It was great fun and before we knew it, we were home!

It was nearly midday, wonderful smells of Christmas food cooking, wafted through the house making us feel ravenous. We would actually be having chicken, a real treat with roast potatoes...I was not so keen on greens, but everything else 'yummy!'

Oh! I nearly forgot that there would also be sage and onion stuffing! Chicken for Christmas Dinner...we couldn't wait.

Most people did not eat chicken in those days not even at Christmas it was a real luxury item. Unbeknown to us, Grandfather had reduced the chicken numbers from the yard! Although he bred them for the table and to provide eggs we thought of them as our pets. I'm sure that if Billy and I had realised, we probably wouldn't have eaten it, luxury or not! But, the mere thought of the succulent white meat, roasted potatoes, stuffing and lovely gravy, made our mouths water.

Granny had also made sausages during Christmas week she was such a good cook. We'd watched her put the sausage meat mixture into the skin, which got longer and longer before she twisted them into individual sausages.

The delicious smell of the food cooking made us so hungry that we started to pester Mum for something to eat. We still had a long wait yet, so Mum relented and allowed us to have a slice of bread and dripping each.

Everyone was ready, Auntie May had her Henna red hair in a roll, with a flower in one side and a lovely green dress. Granddad had a crisp white shirt with a freshly starched collar buttoned on, his best suit and tie, also his gold pocket watch and chain in his waistcoat.

Grandfather, not only in our eyes, but in fact, was a giant at 6ft. 5 inches tall! When he was in the front or back parlour with their high ceilings, he could stand straight, but in the kitchenette or scullery where the ceilings were low, he would constantly have to duck to avoid hitting the lights. By contrast Granny was small, around 5ft and her build was slight; she had the most wonderful wavy dark hair, looking elegant always even after years of drudgery, she'd worked hard all her life. She'd been in Service before marrying Grandfather, working for a rich titled family who lived in the West End, running the house and making sure the other servants knew their daily duties.

Although, the East End was delightfully 'caw-blimey' and 'ows-ya-favver' with always plenty of friendly street-market back-slang and 'ow-ar-ya missus'...Gran' was very much a well-spoken lady, who knew all about etiquette, insisted on good manners and her soft spoken voice, never once raised in anger if we were naughty.

But, if we did play-up she would give us a 'piercing look' that could instantly stop you in your tracks! She was also still very pretty and later as the years began to bend her back with her hands becoming buckled and twisted with arthritis, she never complained; always standing as upright as possible with her head high, proud, stoic and strong...holding the family together no matter what the crisis.

Amazingly, even when she could no longer open her fingers, she would still bake the bread and cakes each week and cook a good meal, every day!

Aunt Ann would be coming for dinner on Christmas Day, coming with Uncle Fred and their new baby girl... my new cousin!

They would be arriving any time now, as it was approaching 3pm, dinner was due to be dished at 4pm.

Mum and Granny were ready too, but still wearing their aprons, which covered the whole of their best frocks. Mum had made them both new aprons, just before Christmas out of some old dresses.

All the women wore these aprons, they were long with a front opening which you put your arms through, then the side sections folded round with ties, tied at the back around the waist.

I was the last to be completely ready.

"When's my hair going to be done, mummy?" I kept moaning.

Mum finally started to remove the strips of rag tied in my hair, and made the curls into ringlets. She parted my hair in the centre, then secured each side with a big pink bow, it was just the perfect style for 'head tossing' and I immediately began prancing about being very irritating, pretending to be a princess one minute, then a royal guard the next. "Anneka...will you stop that noise!"

I suppose it was must have been annoying, I'd been blowing a pretend trumpet for an endless time!

Everyone usually called me 'Annie'...and Mum would only call me Anneka if I'd made her cross!

I sulked off into the corner, wondering why grown-ups didn't understand anything about fun...it was another of life's mysteries?

Billy and I then decided we would play with the cat. He was called 'Tiger' on account of his stripes...he'd only got one eye! Poor thing just came home like it one day, after a bombing raid...he's was fine now, but his one-eye was a great excuse to make out he was a 'pirate cat' putting a black eye patch on him; he didn't seem to mind, that is until we tried to make him wear a pirate hat, made out of newspaper!

He hissed and lashed out at high speed at the newspaper as it fell around his face, running off whilst still hissing as the paper tangled around his body. Wickedly, we laughed and laughed, trying to catch him, as he finally escaped through the scullery window and over the back wall into the barrel arches, leaving scraps of newspaper as he went.

The house was now becoming busier and busier...the table had already been laid today in the front parlour. It would be the first proper Christmas sit-down meal since before the war and a new experience for us. The table had been put in the centre of the room, with the leaf sections opened out to full length with a carver chair at each end for Nan and Granddad and eight other place settings.

The double doors had been opened into the back parlour to make one large room with the thick drapes tied back each side of the large door opening. Grandfather had lit fires in the fireplaces of both rooms. The flames were now licking up and around the chimney, but would soon settle into a glowing mass, keeping the rooms warm.

Uncle John had been sulking upstairs for most of the day because he wanted to go and see his girlfriend Mary, but Granddad wouldn't allow it saying...

"Just remember, Son...you're still young yet...plenty of time for love...she'll wait! Anyway, it's already arranged that she'll be coming this evening with the rest of her family...so be patient!"

We knew that Dad and Uncle George would not be home until sometime in the New Year, but everyone was hopeful that Uncle Bill would make it back for Christmas, but as it was now nearing 4pm a hint of disappointment coloured the atmosphere.

Just as everyone had washed up ready to sit to the table, the front door burst open and in bounced Uncle Bill, throwing down his huge rucksack...rushing through the hall towards the kitchenette, calling out "Mum, Pop....it's me, Bill!"

Grandfather dashed out from the front room, shaking his hands and banging him on the back...then giving him big, manly type hugs!

"Ow are ya, Boy....it's good to see yer!" His voice sounding choked.

Granny was crying and laughing, as Uncle Bill swept her up off her feet and swung her round like a dolly!

He was tall, like Granddad, and when he finally put Nan down, she craned her neck to look at his face, which was now covered with a hairy black beard.

"Have I got time to wash up, shave and change?"

"That's not a problem, Son...I'll just delay dinner 'til you're ready!"

Gran' replied, wiping her eyes.

It was around 5pm when we finally sat down to eat, but it didn't matter...Nan and Granddad was each end of the table, then on one side of the table was Aunt Ann with Uncle Fred, Uncle John and Uncle Bill. On the other side was Auntie May, Billy next to her, then me, and then Mum.

We couldn't believe our eyes...a whole chicken put at one end of the table, then another whole chicken at the other end!

Each had sausages and stuffing on the serving plates, and other dishes with roast potatoes, peas, carrots and spinach, even Yorkshire pudding...what a feast!

"Oh! Nan...do you think the King, Queen and their daughters will have food as good as this?" I asked, not really imagining that anyone could have food like this, anywhere in the world!

Gran' replied with a big smile...

"Well, the Royal family would probably have had Turkey, or maybe Pheasant!" We said 'Grace' before eating, then Granddad and Uncle Bill carved the meat, everything was served. There was a hush as we all began to eat, then the grown-ups began talking about this and that. I was too busy eating to notice what they were talking about!

Although, there was Christmas Pudding and custard for desert, by the end of the meal, nobody had room left to eat it. As everyone wanted to talk at the table after eating, Billy and I were not allowed to get down, which was very frustrating for us 'small people!' Billy began kicking me under the table just for amusement.

Uncle Bill had always been sought after by the ladies, nearly every photograph he'd sent home during the war years, was of him with different girls, making a great fuss of him. They'd even send him perfumed letters and presents, to the constant envy of Uncle George! But, Bill was never serious about any of them, especially when he met a woman called Betty whilst home on one of his 'leave' passes, after that he only had eyes for her!

They all started to laugh when Uncle Bill said

"Hey Dad...do you remember that time I over-stayed my leave?"

There was a momentary hush, as Granddad pulled a big white handkerchief from his pocket and wiped it across his brow saying...

"Remember...how could anyone forget it...you nearly gave us all heart failure?"

Aunt Ann broke in "what's all this about...I never knew anything about it!"

Grandfather began to tell the story, giving a little cough before he started.

"It was a couple of years back now...Bill was home 'on leave' and, as far as we're concerned, not due back for another week! Early one morning Bill gets himself all spruced up and his hair slicked back with Brilliantine to meet Betty, when I notices these official blokes approaching the front door...fortunately, I was late going for the paper!

I guessed it was something to do with Bill, so I shuts the door and shouts to him...'ere you in some sort of trouble?'

Bill makes a bolt for the back...when mother shouts...' Oh! God...it's look like Police coming over the back wall from the arches...what's happening!'

Bill, then bolts up the stairs and gets under one of the beds, closely followed by yer Mother, who jumps in the bed, fully clothed, and covers 'erself up!

I opened the door to try and front it out, and before I can speak they say

'Bill Symmonds, we've got an 'Arrest Warrant' - he's been reported 'Absent without Leave'...and walks in!

Meanwhile, men were also coming in the back door, taking the place apart looking for Bill.

When they starts going up the stairs...I'm telling them...'ere you can't go up there...and, they take no notice, searching every room as they go...'course, when they get to our bedroom door, I'm saying...yer can't go in there, my Wife's very ill!

In they go...huh!...should 'ave seen 'im...covered from head to toe, in white fluff...as they dragged 'im out from under the bed, down the stairs and out the door 'cuffed' for all to see...looking like the 'abominable Snowman'...do I remember?"

Granddad told the story with a 'dead-pan' face, his dry sense of humour 'ringing out the yarn 'for all it was worth, before everyone burst out laughing...it was the first time we'd heard the story, but it wasn't the last.

Granddad told the story about Uncle Bill over-staying his leave many times after that, it was thereafter his guaranteed party piece. Grandfather was excellent at telling stories, you never got tired of hearing them, he could tell the same story with an added slant that made you feel you were hearing it for the first time, every time! He loved to tell jokes too, and he knew absolutely loads.

Everyone could afford to laugh at this story now the War was over but, at the time it was very serious, those few extra days, nearly cost Bill is life as they put him in prison in Chatham; then afterwards they put him on the D.E.M.S (Defensively Equipped Merchant Ships)...crossing back and forth to Ireland in heavily 'mined' waters, he'd thought many times he wouldn't survive those trips!

When we were older and other cousins came along...

Granny Symmonds holding my Cousin Terri

...Granddad would tell us all stories about the 1914/18 War. He told stories about Leprechauns, spooky tales of the wailing omens of the Banshees that came to foretell death in the house. We'd sit spellbound, with our eyes getting wider, open mouthed and all of us snuggling closer together, for security.

We'd go up to bed, jumping at the slightest noise, checking behind the doors and under the beds, scared of every shadow, but we enjoyed it! When we weren't scared anymore, we'd drive him mad to tell us the stories again.

He told of us of how in World War I, he'd have to stand guard during the night outside the mortuary, banging 3 times on the door every 15 minutes, to keep the rats away from the dead bodies. One night, a particularly dark night while on guard duty, he started to hear strange rustling sounds in the bushes...

"Halt! Who goes there?" he'd said.

The noise stopped. A while later the noises came again, this time with a sort of moaning sound, whilst aiming his rifle towards the direction it was coming from.

"Halt, who goes there?"

The noise stopped, with no reply. A while past, then again the noises and the moaning started, this time he became aware of a white shadowy figure, with a long white beard...a creature with white demonic horns approaching him. He brought up his rifle, with his heart pounding in his chest...

"Halt! Who goes there?"

By then, we'd all begun to interrupt...

'Was it a ghost, Granddad?

Did it disappear?

What happened...did you faint?'

"Shall I tell you, kids...well...it got closer until I was just about ready to shoot at the enemy. Sure enough, as it came nearer I knew then...what the white demon was!

There was a clip-clop noise...suddenly there stood a huge 'Billy Goat Gruff!"

We all breathed out a sigh of relief!

On another occasion he told us about a different time...while he was on guard duty...'that a dead man came to life!' He'd been on guard duty for most of the night, doing the usual banging 3 times on the mortuary door.

Suddenly, whilst all his nerves were in a state of awareness and readiness for any approaching enemy... he'd heard strange noises, movements and groaning inside the Mortuary?

He banged the door again, the customary 3 times... when suddenly a voice shouted out...from all places, the voice came from behind the mortuary door?

But...there were only the dead bodies in the Mortuary...Granddad confirmed, how could it be?

He banged 3 times more...a voice shouted...

"Can't a man get a bit of peace?"

We drew breath...in anticipation of what he would say next; imagining a lurching mutilated 'walking dead man, dripping blood and gore' getting up from a slab with outstretched arms, ready to claim a victim!

When we'd held our breath long enough...he told us, it was a 'drunken soldier' who'd gone in there to sleep off the 'booze!' Phew!

Granny decided to clear away the table, before their other visitors came...everyone mucked in to take everything from the table to the kitchenette and Scullery.

Mum started to wash-up, Gran and Auntie May took the rest of the chicken off the bones to store in the safe. The chicken bones were then put in a large pot of water on the kitchen range, to make soup for Boxing Day.

All the men stayed in the two front parlour rooms. They shifted the table back into the bay window, and rearranged the chairs and began discussing all kinds of grown-up men only issues. There was talk of a Wedding too? We wondered what it was all about!

Billy and I had been listening behind the door, giggling...

"Grown-ups are strange, Billy...I don't know whether I want to be a grown-up!"

I declared.

Now evening, the front door was left on the latch and the constant stream of visitors through the house, talked and laughed then turned to a party throng by around 8pm. Uncle Bill had fetched Betty with her two little boys! It was the first time the family had met her and there was some surprise that she had sons, but for us it was wonderful. They were the same age as us, so after learning their names were Arthur and Allen we took them off to show them all around the house asking them constant questions. They told us that their Daddy had left when they were babies and Uncle Bill was going to be their Daddy now!

Uncle John's girlfriend, Mary had also arrived with her family, bringing goodies to the party, even some lemonade.

True to his word 'Tug' had somehow managed to get hold of three large barrels of beer which had been stood on upturned crates along the hallway, also a bottle of Port and a bottle of Johnnie Walker.

Everyone sung endless songs and danced...for the rest of Christmas Day evening. We must have eventually faded off to sleep and been carried up to bed, as the next we knew it was Boxing Day.

"Oh! Wasn't it all wonderful...Billy...wonder what we'll do today?"

Boxing Day was just as full of happy partying and wonderment for us. It was the first of many wonderful Christmas' at 7 Cantrell Road, especially after our Dad was home.

Chapter Nine

New Year, 1946 brought fresh expectations of better times to come, but in reality the home front was still very depressed. I was excited about the prospect of starting school at Easter, when it was also expected that Dad and Uncle George would be back home in England.

Being a rather 'old fashioned' 5 year old I was now allowed to do simple jobs, and particularly liked preparing the salt. Granny kept the salt in a brown earthenware pot on a shelf in the scullery, but first it had to be crushed. The salt came in a block, about the size of a packet of cream crackers, wrapped in white and blue paper called 'XL Salt.' We'd open out the paper, Gran' would cut it into big chunks and I would roll it with a rolling pin 'til it was fine grains then it was put in the earthenware pot.

Sometimes, I could help with the baking too and Granny would explain everything as she went. I'd also help with the washing up, a job I wasn't so fond of as there wasn't 'washing up liquid' in those days, just large soda crystals put in the hot water which made the water feel slippery, even when freshly prepared!

I'd also help with the treasured bits of silverware, cleaned with ash, then polished.

Although we had a small grocery shop close by on the corner of Bow Common Lane and Lockhart Street, we would nearly always take a trip to the shops in Burdett Road. All along Burdett Road outside the shops, the market stalls would set up in the early hours of the morning staying 'til late at night, as late as 11pm or even midnight now it was the run up to Easter.

I'd beg to go late night shopping with Mum and Gran' when they could get extra bargains. As we got closer to the main road you could hear the stallholders' voices, calling out their wares. The light from the lamps, casting eerie moving shadows, as they swung from the corners of the stalls. Sometimes we'd go to Crisp Street market, especially if we needed to get an 'exchange light bulb' from the Electric Office which was near the market, in East India Dock Road. For me it was a very long walk, a good few miles! I rarely managed to walk there and back; climbing into the pushchair with the shopping on the way home.

Uncle John had already started work as an apprentice cabinet maker in Dalston, and Uncle Bill had returned to his former trade as a floor layer. He'd recently started a long contract in the Royal London Hospital in Whitechapel where John Merrick, the Elephant Man had lived in the Victorian era.

Whitechapel of course, being the famous 'killing ground' of Jack the Ripper's unsolved murders of prostitutes.

Uncle Bill had been down in the basement area of the Hospital where all the medical specimens were kept, he'd seen the head of the 'Elephant Man' and other strange things like deformed babies and Siamese Twins that had died at birth, pieces of human anatomy which were stored in huge jars and became the source of many exciting tales.

Other than playing games, stories formed a large part of daily entertainment and anything to do with Whitechapel and the famous Royal London Hospital was to become my first real introduction to history. With a strange marriage to science, stirring in me an unquenchable fascination with endless questions and a search for answers.

Grandfather was a great historian, over the years I learnt so much from his telling of stories about the evolvement of Medicine and all about 'Body Snatchers'.

The Body Snatchers had special relevance for me as we lived directly opposite the oldest part of the Cemetery where we'd often play by gaining access through the missing railings.

The strangest thing of all, in my ponderings about 'medical science' and 'body snatchers' was when I realised that the Cemetery directly opposite our house, went from across the road in Cantrell Road to cover a vast area, meeting with the rear entrance of the Royal London Hospital, St. Clements!

My secret imaginings was of the sick and dying of the hospital; in death, being taken out and buried in the cemetery behind, where immediately these same bodies would be pulled out by the 'body snatchers' and shunted back into the same hospital…to be dissected! All very bizarre!

Death…to a small person, had no real or tangible meaning, it just seemed to me that people simply disappeared!

Where did they go?

Forthcoming explanations of….'if a person is good, they went to a place called Heaven, but if they were bad, they went to Hell seemed to me to be all very unfair!

Needless to say, I was quickly ignored whenever I put my hand up at Sunday school because I'd made this very statement and would ask very unpopular questions. My endless wonderings about this was later to cause me much confusion, especially as our household held very religious beliefs, Gran in particular being an unquestionably devout Catholic.

I'd so wanted to ask one day, when I'd heard a disturbing story...that the Devil had once been God's right hand Angel, but they'd had a serious disagreement!

Why, had they had a row?

Why hadn't God forgiven his chief angel?

Why had God created such a terrible place called Hell, with burning fires and damnation; giving the Devil the job of running it, and tempting mere mortals to Sin?

Did animals go to Heaven or Hell?

Mysteries! Confusing mysteries to try and fathom?'

Auntie May, Grandad's sister had so looked forward to her birthday in February, 1946 when she would be 60 years old, retiring from her work. I'd always enjoyed spending time with her, she would often do my hair and let me put her perfume on or take me with her shopping. She always had a lovely sweet flowery smell about her and her powdered face was soft and smooth. She wore very smart clothes, although they'd become old and worn they still looked good, also she'd wear an assortment of strange shaped hats that really suited her.

She'd moved in with Gran' and Granddad many years prior to the war, after her husband died of Tuberculosis, and after her baby died at birth. She was never interested in meeting or remarrying anyone else. Mum made

Auntie a 60th Birthday cake and we all had a small celebration, whilst she sat telling everyone plans for retirement, which sadly it wasn't to be.

Around a week or so after Auntie's birthday, she'd gone off to bed early complaining of indigestion whilst the rest of us sat in the warm kitchenette. Suddenly, I was aware that whilst everyone was quiet I could hear strange sounds!

Mum said "It's probably one of the boys coming home!"

Bill and John had gone out for the evening.

Granddad checked the hallway, but nobody was there.

Billy and I huddled together as we'd sensed the atmosphere was foreboding...there came more strange noises and Granddad looked straight up at the large picture of his parents hanging on the wall, where the sounds now seemed to be coming from; turning to look across to Gran'...she immediately clutched her chest!

"Oh! George...it's the Banshees!"

The sounds continued and Mum decided to go and check on Auntie with me following, hanging on a piece of her skirt. Breathing a sigh of relief, to see she was sleeping and looked fine. But, the sounds from the area of the picture did not stop until around midnight...I'd burst into tears at one point and refused to go to bed, so did Billy! Everyone convinced of it being the banshees foretelling of a death in the house, we'd all finally got to bed. Whether strange, fact or fiction...our beloved Auntie May was gone. She'd passed away peacefully in her sleep during that night!

Her funeral would be traditional as far as Grandfather was concerned the 'send-off' for his sister would be the best possible affair. And, as it was for Royalty, the 'laying in state' so it would be for Auntie May.

She'd left a Will, with everything going to Grandfather also a 'Penny Life Policy' and some savings, which would more than cover the funeral expenses. The front and back parlour rooms were opened out, and Auntie was embalmed, dressed in white silk and laid in a beautiful casket with brass handles.

Saddened that I would not be spending time talking with her anymore, I would go and sit with her in the front room. As was the tradition, someone sat with her by taking it in turns, so she was never alone. She looked so lovely, just as though she was asleep with the feint appearance of a smile; although young and previously in awe of death, it was to leave me with a memory of comfort that she appeared happy in her 'passing' as she'd been in life.

The 'wake' had begun...the house kept in quiet, no radio and always people spoke softly almost in whispers. Beautiful little white cards with black shaped edges were printed, showing the date of Auntie's funeral and 'Order of Service' also a verse on the back, were posted or given out. On the day of the funeral, everyone wore black and heads had to be covered. Outside the house came the Horse-drawn Hearse, the horses had tall white plumes on their heads, and the men wore Top Hats and long black coats. The coffin was placed inside the carriage and the flowers put on top, I'd never seen so many flowers and wreaths; it was the first funeral Billy and I had ever witnessed.

The carriage was very grand, with sectioned windows of glistening glass and patterns engraved on them, and the black wood and brass, highly polished.

Food had been prepared on the morning of the funeral, for when everyone returned after the service. The funeral's procession started out with a sombre march, moving off slowly from the house with the mourners, friends and neighbours walking 'heads bowed' behind, displaying heartfelt solemn respect.

Upon their return it was very acceptable, indeed even required, that following a funeral events became a celebration of the person's life, and a party in their honour! The more happy stories, jokes in good taste about the person being 'sent off' and laughter, the better!

The celebration after Auntie May's funeral was everything and more, the kind of party she would have approved of, leaving me with a lasting impression, that a 'send-off' for someone 'loved' should be like this one! I would miss Auntie May always, but it wasn't sad anymore.

As the weeks passed, happier times again came to the fore as during March both Dad and Uncle George arrived home, within days of each other. We enjoyed Easter as a family and everyone made preparation for a Spring Wedding, Uncle Bill to Betty.

Dad later took over the sole running of his father's building company. He'd worked with his father before the war, hence the name of Oakes & Son Builders.

George loved to be outside on the water and eventually got his own barge, working and maintaining the Grand Union and Regents Canals travelling back and forth.

Sometimes, he would go out with Granddad and 'Tug' on the Thames.

Billy and I had not previously seen much of the 'Oakes' family, but now we saw quite a lot of Dad's young brother, Donald. He was around the same age as

Mum's brother, John and they became good friends. Don came to Gran and Granddad's several times a week to see John. They stayed mates over the years, going to Pubs together, as they got older.

The house was now full, always busy and happy.

But, in the early days after Dad and George's return, for some time they both seemed tense and edgy. They'd been on some of the same missions together and as Commandos they understood each other's experiences of war, the training, the camaraderie and their secret problems of returning to civilian life. They could only openly discuss these things with each other, often going into the front room together, sitting for hours talking. Being a curious little person, I always wanted to know what they talked about!

Mum said when I badgered her...

"It's grown-up men's talk, and not for small people to know!"

My curiosity was always bound to drive me to naughtiness eventually, simply had to know...

Chapter Ten

L ate one night, I awoke...the house was in darkness 'it must be late' I thought! But, I was aware of muffled sounds of voices downstairs. Creeping as quietly as possible to the bedroom door, I opened it slowly...

"What are you doing, Sis'...?" Billy asked.

"Hush Billy, I want to hear what's being said downstairs. I think Dad's talking to Uncle George!"

"I'm coming too!" Billy announced.

"No, if we both go, we're bound to get caught!"

There was no putting him off...

"Alright, but you must be very quiet...as a mouse!"

We made our way down the stairs, stopping instantly if one of the stairs started to creak...eventually reaching the door of the front parlour, sitting ourselves one each side the door. I gestured across to Billy, with my finger up to my mouth, to be quiet. Where we first heard Uncle George speaking....

"You'll never believe who I bumped into today, Bill? Jimmy Weidner...Yeah! He looked well...good to see him. I really thought he was a gonna! I'd asked around if anyone had seen him a number of times, but nobody knew anything, or seen him! Strange thing...I came across a Canadian chap, called Weidner during the war!

Remember me telling you, Bill...? Jimmy Weidner, yeah! He volunteered as a Royal Marine Commando, and went off to Achnacarry for training, not long after I'd become an RNC. Anyway, I was walking along the Mile End Road, when there he was, large as life and looking great. He was telling me...he'd been on the Normandy landings that went in onto Sword Beach on D-Day... with your lot Bill, the No. 4's and the two French troops of 10 (Inter-Allied) Commando.

Bloody amazing...the size of the D-Day Landings and he should go in on the same beach to move on to Ouistreham and the Benouville Bridge to join the 6th Airborne...and get caught up in the same severe hand-to-hand fighting, as you! Jim had taken his party of men in to land on Sword Beach...in the landing craft...and been in the 'thick of it!' A lot of his mates 'copped it' during that landing; said he couldn't believe he'd made it through.

None of us could, though...you know that, Bill... none of us could!

When he got on to Sword Beach there was intense fire that already had the 8th Brigade pinned, down coming from a pillbox 'til the Commando pushed through and took it. It's a funny thing, strange really, but...he was saying the same as us...he doesn't talk about it at home!

He's getting married to one of the 'Barwick' family, remember Bill; the big family of 11 children. Our Bill used to go to school with Alec Barwick...!

Bye the way, they're still waiting for Alec to come home from Burma...he's out there still, like cousin Whalley Symmonds....his letters tell a bad story of jungle warfare, and the Japanese! Not that many letters have got through! Yeah!...Jim's just got engaged to

Patricia Barwick...such a small world really...you must remember Pat, the dark-haired 'stunner' that came here once with your Sister Sally.

They'd met and become friends when they both joined up at the same time in the W.A.A.F. in 1942. Jim said Pat was all he thought about, and worried about... while he was away on missions during the war. Her letters, when he got them...kept him going!

I was pleased not to have a girlfriend or wife, Bill! In all honesty...for me it would have been one more thing to worry about at least I was only concerned with what happened to the family.

Those Landings were a bastard, especially Italy, having to probe about with our F-S daggers...wondering when you'd 'get it!'

I saw it happen to a bloke once...bits of him, flew everywhere.

We had to carry on...he may have even been washed out with the tide. There was only a bit of a lull...after the fall of Sicily, Mussolini was 'ousted' from power as the result of a palace revolution on the 25th July, 1943... King Victor Emmanuel II confided the government to Marshall Badoglio.

Got to have been hard for the Italians already here... 'Old Dick Di Costa' was a good mate of mine...don't know what happened to him, after his 'Chippie' was bombed? Used to enjoy popping round the corner to get fish and chips on a Saturday night! Officially, of course, the Badoglio government continued to support the German cause, but it was evident that Italy, at that time, was on the verge of surrender. Yeah! They stuck Mussolini in a Hotel which was inaccessible, and kept him imprisoned there in the Gran Sasso. Badoglio, opened negotiations with the Allies via captured British General Carton de Wiart.

We'd heard that American, British and Italian representatives met in Lisbon and an Armistice was later signed at Syracuse on the 3rd September, the very day we'd landed at Reggio in Calabria. As the Germans had been expecting the defection of their Italian Allies, they acted promptly and seized Rome. The King, with Badoglio just managed to slip through the German net with difficulty. Much of the Italian fleet, including four battleships and six cruisers, sailed to Malta and surrendered in early September. With the Italians out of the way the British landings at Reggio and the seizure of Taranto on the 9th September weren't contested. But, it wasn't so hot for the US Fifth Army who'd landed that day in the Gulf of Salerno, nor for us come to that...we had to neutralise the minefields!

Anzio was bloody awful, especially trying to deal with those 'wood encased mines'.

You know...that Monastery at Monte Cassino was unbelievable it dominated the whole battlefield of the Liri Valley.

I made a point of finding out about that Monastery! Amazing, it was founded by St. Benedict in 529 AD. Before the Second World War it was a place of pilgrimage, of universal learning having a massive library and archives. Fortunately they were all transferred to the Vatican at the beginning of the war, but the Monks remained.

When the Germans came to fortify the area around Cassino, the Monastery offered a good observation point to command the ground. It became a real obsession with the Allied Commanders in 1944. Bloody shame really, it was bombed heavily in March '44, but fighting continued 'til May, when the position was finally taken by the Polish Troops. Strange thing Bill...I couldn't believe we'd both end up at Walcheren!"

There was a silence for a while...

Then Dad's distinctive voice could be heard...

"Yeah!...Hitler's Commando Order in October, 1942 made everyone sharp, George...after that fiasco on the Island of Sark...unfortunate business!

It could have happened to anyone acting in the heat of the moment. They'd captured those Germans and tied their hands behind their backs...only shooting them after they'd started screaming out. If they hadn't have shot 'em, it could have resulted in our boys being killed, especially if the enemy had been alerted! It seems to me, there wasn't time to quieten them any other way?

It certainly made us all determined 'never to be taken prisoner by the Germans, knowing you'd be immediately executed!' As far as Hitler was concerned, Commandos were all murderers, gangsters and low-life criminals!

You can bet though, George...those Germans must have wondered what was coming at them when they heard those bagpipes and witnessed Mad Jack Churchill going into battle waving his 'Highland Broadsword' over his head...what a sight!

Gotta laugh really, George!

The only thing stopping Hitler's Order to execute Commandos, whether in uniform or not, being bloody hysterical, is that some really good men actually 'got it!'

Some of the Free French that had been with us, just disappeared on a reconnaissance one time, George...it was about 2 years before we'd learnt that the Germans had captured and executed them!

Then there was the Commando Troop, nicknamed the 'Cockleshell Heroes' some of them were captured and executed, just shot...doing their job for King and Country! But, you're right in what you've said I found it hard worrying about a wife and kids, George. And, how do undo all this stuff in your head...one minute your trained as an 'elite killing machine' then the next, you're expected to become 'an average Joe?'

Glad's often asked me questions about our missions, George, but how can I tell her, the sort of things I've seen, and had to do?

She would never see me in the same light again! I don't know about you, but I find it hard sometimes to get the images out of my mind...I certainly thought I'd 'get it' at Dieppe. As we came in to the beaches...and in quick succession it came to me to get off the landing craft...down I go! As you know George, there's little time to think, you just do what you're trained to do... I go down under the water into a shell hole, with the back-pack dragging and pinning me down.

The pain in my chest was unbearable, my lungs about to burst as I'm wrestling to get the pack off...weighing twice as much under the water. God knows! I thought I was a 'gonna' there an' then.

Just as I thought I'd pass out any second, it came free...I practically shot out of the water, dragging in air, for all I was worth. Now I'm running up the beach, gasping for air still, with no pack and no weapon! Christ, George...there was no shortage of replacements, bodies were everywhere!

I grabbed a pack off one of the dead...and a Bren, finding myself running alongside one of our Troop. I didn't notice who it was, but almost as soon as I was aware of him there, than a sharp sound of a crack took his head clean off...his legs taking several steps before dropping!

God...the shock made me question for a second or so, whether I was dead as well...how, could I still be alive?

I swear George there wasn't even a tear in my uniform...

I continued to run up the beach; I could even feel his blood's warmth for a while with pieces of him dropping off me, as I went.

That last leave before Walcheren was the hardest 14 days...I tried to give Glad a nice time, but I couldn't unwind. So many flashbacks! So much horror!

We went to the Pictures, can't even remember the film, I was too restless...and as for the bloody newsreels with pictures of battlefronts and screaming shells, I just wanted to walk out!

I don't know George, but I think Glad was confused by my distance, and she couldn't fathom why I seemed so different!

But, I couldn't explain to her...didn't know myself... was just ill at ease, on edge!

When I got back to Petworth...I fell back into the old 'automatic' routine of 'joking around with the guys' especially with Eddie Oates...having similar names, gave us the perfect excuse to rib each other. There was a bunch of us that stuck together a lot of the time... Anthony Doubler who came from Cardiff, William Hegarty from Paddington, Willie Kirby, he came from Clapton and there was William Rowse from Swansea, who for some strange reason everyone called 'Mike'.

Although the French chaps would normally stick around together, Francois Navarro who originally came from the Sevres area of France used to spend a bit of time with us. I liked him a lot enjoyed chatting to him about his home and his family.

We were told that we would probably be sent to the Far East when we attended the lectures on jungle warfare, being told the difference between the War we'd experienced and the one we would see. But, suddenly we received the movement order, not as expected to the Far East, but back to France.

On the 6th October, crossed from Newhaven to Dieppe...then moving on into Belgium. We moved into billets in little place called den Haan, near Ostende to begin training...McVeigh was now a sergeant. Rowse as C.S.M., and some of the chaps wounded during D-Day were back. As yet we hadn't been told what our next task would be, but the haste of our movement suggested that something was about to happen, we were all a bit tense. But, we set about getting fit with cross-country runs, field-firing exercises, sometimes playing football.

The war by now had pushed well into Belgium and far as the German frontiers with the enemy holding out around the estuary of the Scheldt, still controlling a large part of Holland. In the third week of October a hint of our task had reached us. We were to be given a direct assault on a heavily defended area! Our Troop leader informed us that street-fighting would be on the cards and to prepare accordingly. We continued training in an area in the outskirts of Ostende...clambering up and down walls using toggle-ropes, moving through the rows of houses. Crossing open spaces using smoke grenades. The following week we were finally told that our objective was Flushing, the port of the island of Walcheren. The Germans had apparently spent four years fortifying the place but, the R.A.F. had breached the main sea dykes on the island in two places, one outside Flushing.

Flushing itself falls into two parts, the old dock area and the newer, more residential part, separated by a section of land about four hundred yards wide, where there are two main road junctions. These main road junctions connect the old and the new sections of the town. The idea was for us to land, push straight through the old part of the town and seize these two road junctions, hold and clear them, for follow-up troops to then push through into the new part. It was clear that the difficulty would lay in getting ashore, with the sea wall itself a complete obstacle to any sea borne assault, while every possible landing area being exposed by a system of supporting strongpoints and pill-boxes.

The silence was deafening, faces were gloomy... everyone knew that although things rarely turned out as first planned, the odds in this assault plan was so heavily stacked in favour of the enemy that it was inevitable that casualties would be heavy.

The only chance we could take advantage of was to land in darkness, and try to rush the obstacles.

George, you know the feeling just before a mission, it's indescribable...

I thought of home, of Gladys, wondering whether I would make it back! How she'd cope if I didn't!

I turned to Doubler and Hegarty, we all knew we felt depressed, it didn't need to be said...I made some vague attempt at a joke...but, couldn't help thinking of those we'd already lost in previous raids, friends and great blokes!

The plan for the assault hinged on the initial landing and if the landings were successful, there was a reasonable chance that the whole Commando could get ashore and striking their objectives before the Garrison had realised a landing in any strength had happened. The R.A.F. would also being bombing the Garrison.

Moving on to Breskens on the last day of October, Breskens had been badly battered and hardly resembled a town, and the little harbour which was also damaged, hardly usable...lay our landing craft. The usual taut and flat heavy feeling was not helped by enemy shelling of the area behind Breskens.

We tried to get some rest, but slept uneasy, being roused 2.45am. Matters was made worse by the news that the bombing had to be cancelled, owing to bad flying conditions...the air was blue with much cursing of the R.A.F., before we headed off to the harbour to embark. It was 04-40 hours, with Denny Rewcastle and his section the first to slip out of the harbour having the uneviable task of finding a place to land, as no landing place had been fixed! It was Denny's job to find an area capable of landing then clearing the area around the landing point, to hang on there, establishing a small bridgehead and signal the rest of us.

The pressure on him must have been immense, as upon his decision hinged the success or failure of the whole operation. Within minutes of Denny's departure the immense din of the barrage begun, with the remaining craft just clearing the harbour entrance. Fires could be seen in the town across the water, the shells screamed overhead, the explosions reverberating.

Everyone's faces, ears and necks were carefully smeared with sooty camouflage, and the flashes of the bursts of fire from the shoreline would occasionally catch a glint of someone's eyes in the otherwise shapeless faces. Drizzling fine rain fell as we quietly and anxiously strained our eyes towards the shoreline whilst circling in the landing-craft. Eventually we could just see the landing party touch down where the wooden pier joined the mole. Scrambling ashore, slipping on the wet stonework of the dykes, moving forward to the line of stakes on the side of the mole. The leading man put two stakes a small distance apart, then slipped through, behind him came the next man with a roll of white tape on his belt, unrolling the tape as he went forward marking a safe track to follow.

Then a small group started moving towards the pill-boxes on the mole. We saw the winking light of our signal to move in and whilst still about a couple of hundred yards offshore, a 20-millimetre cannon opened up, firing from the left of us, sending red streaks of tracer that whooshed and cracked only a few feet over the L.C.A., our heads peering up above the sides...then machine-gun fire.

Fortunately, we were low in the water and we prayed the gunners on the shore would continue to fire at normal deck level, their fire passing overhead. By this time the adrenaline's pumping as we're in the last stages of the run-in with the fire fairly heavy. They finally succeeded in sinking two of our L.C.A's only a few yards from the shore with casualties. We just managed to scramble onto the slippery stonework of the mole to follow the white tape, to meet up with the others. The time was now 06.30 hours and the beachhead was now established.

Speed, now of the essence as the initiative lay with us...we hurried along in the half-light! We met with no opposition, but found it unnerving to see dimly lit figures flitting across the streets...not knowing whether they were Germans, or Dutch civilians trying to take refuge! As we threaded our way through the dim streets, running...I was going over in my mind the details of the route from the aerial photographs, continuing on towards the objectives.

From time to time we heard the terrific crash of an explosion the vibrations causing great chunks to fall from some of the houses. Although in our briefing it was agreed that we would not engage any enemy on the way through the town, unless directly between us and our objectives, we were surprised by suddenly coming under fire from bursts of machine-gun fire, which dropped two of our men. Taking cover of the shops and houses, we continued to work our way towards the objectives. One section of men branched off to the left front...Oates was among them...he called out

"See yer later Oakes"

I called back "Not if I see yer first Oates"

It momentarily took the tension out of the air, as I chuckled at our little standing joke! My group branched off to the right towards the barracks and as we moved along I heard sniper fire from the direction of the other group, one of the men was killed instantly. We carried on toward the barracks on the seafront, along an alleyway at the end of which there was small houses. Although we narrowly missed walking directly into a body of German Soldiers, we'd been spotted and the Germans opened fire.

Unbelievably 'Donkin' who was a legend among the Commando being the oldest member at 41 years old, a stocky built ex-miner and father of nine children, soon to be ten...leapt into the doorway, setting both feet firmly in each corner of the door-jamb. Starting to Tommy gun from left to right through maybe 15 or more Germans, but as he begun to swing back his fire from the right, one of the wounded Germans took a shot.

It took Donkin straight through the throat, and killed him instantly.

The enemy knew exactly where we were...reaching the barracks, the men rushed through the building clearing every room...one man kicking open the door would leap in to the far side of the room, whilst another covered the doorway and passage. We finished the remaining rooms engaging pockets of 'fixed bayonet' fighting...petrified for a moment, with my heart pounding...I spotted, just in the nick of time a bayonet point inch forward from the doorway, close by. One thing to shoot a man, but to 'stick' a man is something else...I had no choice, it was him or me! I stood a good chance of surprise if I acted quick...fortunately the doorway was to my right. Grabbing his gun with my left hand and pushing it upwards, lunging the dagger in my right hand...up hard under his ribs with one thrust, and out...it was a sickening feeling, as I felt his last warm gush of breath hit my face.

I swung round fast, checking behind me and called out to Hegarty to cover me whilst I checked the room for other Germans...it was clear.

The others had moved on ahead, we caught up just as a tunnel had been discovered running the whole length of the sea-front with numerous openings on the promenade. The entire length was covered by a machine-gun position on the right...it was impossible for us to get out on the seaward side without becoming a 'sitting target' for the machine-gunner. It would also be possible for the enemy to come along the seaward side behind us, without knowing, cutting us off from the rest of our small group!

The situation wasn't good, then one of the men grabbed one of the German Prisoners, telling him to go out and tell his friends to surrender. The German was reluctant 'til McVeigh's impatience turned to aggression. He rammed his rifle into the man's back and pushed him along, disappearing with him into a house. Some while later, when we all thought he'd been jumped, out he came shouting...

"Here they come Sir!"

We watched as a line of 75 Germans appeared with their hands clasped on their heads.

Fighting was more or less continuous all day, with our machine-gun sections hanging on against counter-attacks as the enemy tried to aide those Germans pinned in the old part of the town. Darkness fell and it was decided to stay put 'til morning with the follow-up troops ashore in strength due to make their thrust the next day into the new part of Flushing and to the batteries on its outskirts. Although the German strongpoint held out stubbornly, we had in support the first aerial cab-rank service of the war. Rocket firing Typhoons which circled overhead... these were called and minutes later they swooped down on the German position in terrifying attacks. It didn't take long for the 'white flag' to appear and some 54 men and 3 German Officers came out, looking very shaken. Next day we left Flushing crossed the breach in the dyke working our way along the dunes to Zoutland where we stayed the night, then travelled on to Domburg. After which we would push through to the last place in enemy hands, Vrouwenpolder. It meant a night march in order to be in a position to attack in the morning...by the end of afternoon, we had 1400 German prisoners, Vrouwenpolder was occupied by the Commando, and the battle of Walcheren was at an end. Resting up for a while, we turned to our tins of self-heating soup and sat talking. Then Hegarty called over...

"Hey, Bill...have you heard what some bright spark reckons...the Germans regard war as a profession, the British as a sport and the Americans as a job, and the uniforms supposedly reflect this! Yeah! The Germans with insignia, badges and leather, the British with baggy comfortable 'Grouse Moor' outdoor clothes and the Americans with workmanlike boots and cotton drill uniforms!"

Laughing, I called back to him...

"Well, that bloke whoever he was...hasn't seen this shabby bunch of Germans!"

No.4 Commando D troop. Flushing.
Photo courtesy of Candice Moore

During the remainder of the Winter of 1944-5 we continued to carry out small-scale raids and patrols amongst the islands of the Scheldt, tactically preventing any German counter-attacks from the north-west against Antwerp. Until March, 1945 we were stationed on North Beveland and patrolled onto the next island. Then we moved on to the mainland, with the end of hostilities finding us near Bergen-op-Zoom.

June, 1945 we moved into Germany to Recklinghausen in the Ruhr, guarding a prison camp. An interrogation team was set up to deal with the two P.O.W. Camps, containing around 250,000 prisoners of different ranks. The interrogation began after they were put into groups seeking out wanted men for War Crime Trials.

Depressing business...some of them had been guards in concentration camps, scarcely men at all really; others were doctors carrying out so-called 'experiments in the cause of science' and as for the S.S. they were still arrogant and thoroughly contemptuous, bastards!

Many of those Germans...George, the average soldiers, were broken bits of humanity in a terrible state with Tuberculosis and Dysentery!

I was over the moon to be returning to England in March, 1946. But, in all honesty, bloody sick that we were officially disbanded...we'd fought together, ate and slept together...we were a brotherhood! We felt choked as we said our 'goodbyes'...must have been the same for you, George?

I wasn't looking forward to going back to my original Army Unit, I'd left years before...who would I know?"

As Dad was still talking about coming home to us, my head suddenly bashed against the door as I fell off to sleep! Jumping in shock and horror at getting caught, decided to creep back to bed. Billy had long been asleep, lying on the floor. I shook him gently, just enough to keep him quiet...we stumbled up the stairs, flopping into bed.

Chapter Eleven

It was a crisp, bright Spring morning as dawn broke. A good few minutes before I remembered being outside the parlour door the night before, listening to Uncle George and Daddy's horrific experiences. Later at breakfast, I stared hard at Dad's face looking into his eyes...he looked back a couple of times, with a puzzled gaze. I felt as though I now held his deepest emotions.

As young as I was, I knew I somehow wanted to make him feel better from what he'd experienced. Sometimes, I'd touch his arm and he'd smile down at me, with a wide warm grin that lit his whole face, and say...

"Okay! Little Doll?" I'd run off giggling!

It seemed that no sooner was our house full, a complete bustling home and family again, people were leaving home again! When Aunt Ann and Fred got married they'd gone to live in Bromley Hall Road. When their baby girl arrived, my cousin, they'd named her Gladys, after Mum. But, as she got older she changed her name to Terri.

Mum said she didn't blame her, she was never overly keen on the name Gladys herself, preferring her second name of Victoria. Uncle Bill married Betty and set up home, taking on Arthur and Allen as his own sons, who really loved him in return. They'd moved to a flat for a while, near Bromley-by-Bow Station and St. Andrew's Hospital, later having three daughters Linda, June and Beverly.

I started school at Devons Road Primary. I wasn't sure that I liked school, as the other kids would pull off my nice 'bobble' hats, that Mummy knitted, and put them down the toilet! Then I'd get a telling off from Mum about it; I'd cover up what was happening by telling her, it was my fault...I'd accidentally dropped them down the lavatory.

Mum would take and collect me from school which always seemed such a long walk! Sometimes, I'd go to school with Janet and her Mum, from No. 10...we'd sit next to each other in school. We both had long hair, put in ringlets each day. Our Mum's were friends 'til one fateful day, when I found a pair of rusty scissors up near the bombed houses. Janet and I decided we would play 'hairdressers!'

We cut off each other's ringlets and tied them on a bush growing up near 'Tug' Wilson's house. The perfect ringlets of different colour hair, we thought, made a great decoration for the bush! Taking it in turns to cut off several ringlets at a time, leaving huge gaps on our heads where the tresses used to be.

All of a sudden, Janet's Mum caught us, and the ensuing pandemonium was horrific...we both burst into great heaving sobs, crying hysterically! She dragged us, by what was left of our hair, along the road still screaming and shouting at us 'til we reached No. 7...calling out for my Mum to come and see....what I'd done to her daughter's hair? My Mum naturally protested...

"well who do you think did 'that' to Annie's hair, if it wasn't 'your' daughter?"

Janet and me...we looked at each other, terrified of what punishment would result? Nothing seemed to get resolved between our respective Mother's probably they wouldn't be such good friends for a while! We'd both have to go to bed each night straight after tea, for at least the next week.

When we got to school the next morning and looked at each other...our mouths dropped open. Janet's Mum had cut the rest of the ringlets off, in chunks! Mum had done the same thing to my hair! The other kids at school pointed and laughed at us....we looked like terrible, wild-eyed Victorian 'street urchins!' Janet and I realised there and then, that our punishment was complete!

The summer months of 1946 were wonderful... Mummy and Daddy would sometimes take us to Victoria Park, we'd have a packed lunch and homemade lemonade. It was a long way to walk, travelling up Bow Common Lane to Burdett Road then crossing the Mile End Road into Grove Road and on to the Park near Old Ford. It seemed vast to small people like us, another world. Billy and I used to think we were in the Country! If we were very lucky Dad would buy us all ice-cream, we'd eat them sitting by the boating lake. Mum and Dad would be giggle and reminisce about when they met.

Other days Billy and I would climb in through the broken railings of the cemetery across the road, which was the old part and overgrown, we'd pretend it was the jungle. We'd also play ballgames in the road, as traffic rarely came along Cantrell Road, and what did, was always horse-drawn 'rag and bone' carts, or the coal man.

Sometimes the ice-cream bike, or the knife sharpener man, who'd also come on a bike with his 'grinding wheel' on the front. Although, Gran' would make 'pie-n-mash' at home, it was a special treat to go and eat at Charles' Eel & Pie House on Burdett Road...for all the years I can remember, it was always packed. It was a family concern, with the matriarch of the business serving and taking the money at the front, and her son Charles Jnr., out back...preparing and cooking the food. The father, Charles Snr., had been killed during the War.

After purchasing our plates of pie-n-mash, we'd go through the doorway into the next part of the shop, sitting at marble topped tables on benches. I liked to sit near the back of the shop as there was an opening through which you could see Charles Jnr., doing the cooking; wiping his brow after getting out large trays of hot pies from the oven. Every so often, you'd hear his Mother shout out "Pies" or "Mash and Eels"...Charles would then, bang a tray of pies, mash, eels or a pot of liquor... through the window opening, appear out of the nearby door and carry the food through to the front counter. Everything to us as children was fun, full of interesting learning.

From the pie shop we'd walk to each individual shop on Burdett Road, the delicatessen where Granny would buy only 'best butter' which came in several grades. The butter was scooped out of a container, weighed, shaped with two flat wooden utensils into an oblong then wrapped in greaseproof paper. Then, we'd go to the butchers to buy meat, faggots or saveloys, moving to the greengrocers shop next for the veg.

Mum and Gran' would weave back and forth from the shops to the market stalls outside, looking for the best prices and quality. Fish-n-chips another rare treat, when we would ask for a bag of 'bits' which was all the pieces of batter that had dropped off the fish when fried. They'd be in a folded piece of newspaper to form a bag, open at the top, we'd sprinkle the 'batter bits' with far too much 'salt and vinegar!' Eating them all the way home, our lips would end up white from the effects of the vinegar. Not the most healthy of foods by today's standards, but...simply delicious!

Autumn came, then winter and we were really looking forward to our first Guy Fawkes night celebration...the bonfires had been built, we would have fireworks, rockets, catherine wheels, bangers and sparklers!

We'd been playing in the street with the other kids, when tragedy struck...it was a frosty Sunday morning, playing football. Billy ran to the centre of the road to pick up the ball....there was a screeching noise, and we all stood transfixed to the spot looking around to see what it was. Suddenly, I looked to the right towards the railway bridge to see a black vehicle roaring through the arch, heading for Billy...I screamed at him, but there was no time for him to react. Still clutching the ball when the vehicle struck him with a loud thud, hurtling him high into the air, somersaulting in what seemed like slow-motion before he landed in the kerb. The vehicle continued on to swerve round the corner into Bow Common Lane, without even stopping!

He lay still, making a slight moan as I ran to him, I screamed for help. I could see that he was badly hurt, with his foot folded round by the side of his leg, jagged bones protruding and blood everywhere. I tried to comfort him by telling him he'd be fine...Mummy and

Daddy would come soon! I pulled his foot round to meet his leg, still attached by only a small amount of skin...it seemed the natural thing to do...as though, perhaps by magic his injury would disappear, but the bones were jutting out like spears.

I pulled out my clean white handkerchief and gently put it over the wound so he wouldn't see, my salty tears dropping on his bare legs, screaming out again for somebody to get help. I was sure my brother would die, desperately trying to control my fear and tears, so as not to frighten him.

Our parents came and Daddy pulled off his belt putting it round his upper leg to stem the flow of blood, he then secured his leg with a piece of wood, whilst Mum brought some bandages. She too was now crying with silent tears flowing down her cheeks. The neighbours offered to help, but there was nothing they could do... nobody had cars or telephones.

Billy hadn't cried or made a sound, except to say he felt cold. Dad seemed to know what to do and wrapping him in his jacket he scooped him up in his arms and started to run with him towards the railway arch in the direction of St. Andrew's Hospital, accompanied by Mum. I was begging to go too, but Gran and Granddad said I would slow them down and I would see Billy later...

"You must come home for now!" Nan insisted

It was a long day that we all sat waiting to hear news of Billy. Breaking into sobs, I stuttered...

"Will Billy die Granddad...God wouldn't take Billy away would he?"

"He'll be fine...you'll see!"

Uncle George decided he'd had enough of the wait

"C'mon Pop, let's get up to St. Andrew's and see what's going on!"

Granddad put on his thick coat, scarf and cloth cap and out they went to find it snowing, a thin layer of snow had already formed on the road and pavement. We were still waiting for news when a knock came...Uncle John answered it to see two Policemen who wanted information about the accident. Gran' was puzzled asking them how they knew about the accident, as she led them to the front room. They explained that they'd been making enquires all that day following a robbery at 'The Widow's Son' public house on Devons Road.

Eye witnesses' had reported seeing the robbers make their getaway in a black Ford van that turned into Knapp Road, leading to us in Cantrell Road. When they spoke to the people in No. 11 which was 'Tug' he'd informed them in no uncertain terms of his outrage that the driver and perpetrator of Billy's injuries, never even stopped!

This was most interesting to the police who wanted to know more about the vehicle, the driver and who else might have been in the van, than how Billy was doing. Gran' let them know of her complete disgust!

Whether in shock...I felt very tired and fell in and out of fit-full sleep in one of the kitchenette armchairs near the warm range. There was a large pot of soup cooking, but everyone was too concerned about Billy to eat. It was now dark, but still early evening when I startled upon hearing Granddad's voice as he came down the hall into the kitchenette with George. Both looking very serious, proceeding to tell Gran' and Uncle John what had been happening at the hospital, with me interrupting in a state of hysteria. The hospital had wanted to amputate Billy's foot, but Dad had insisted they tried anything and everything to save it. Dad's father had done a lot of building work for a Consultant Orthopaedic Surgeon, who lived in London's West End and mainly operated at the London Jewish Hospital, a Mr. Hyman. Dad asked the doctors if, before they operated, he could try and contact him.

St. Andrew's reluctantly agreed, but warned Mum and Dad they could only wait a limited period before they would have to amputate. Mr. Hyman came as soon as he'd heard, arriving with just time to spare. Examining Billy, he'd assured them he'd do his best to save his foot, confident it was possible. The operation took around 5 hours and a metal plate had been put in his leg, then Mr. Hyman arranged for a transfer to the London Jewish Hospital, where his team would look after him, as he would need more operations. Naturally, Billy missed Guy Fawkes night that year, and the forthcoming Christmas celebrations. Although we went to see him often, nothing at home seemed the same without him.

January, 1947 saw the return of the last British soldiers to 'civvy street'...but, for another Auntie who lived in Manor Park, Aunt Bertha, her husband's return would be tinged with sadness. They'd only been wed a few months before the war started and he'd ended up in Burma. By all accounts he was a really jolly chap, light hearted and full of fun, he'd returned a completely changed man, thin, aged, in poor health and morose. His health and attitudes to life improved with time, but he never returned to his former self; Burma had virtually destroyed him.

The rest of the year was very dull as far as I was concerned, I felt lonely and missed Billy. He had to have six operations in all, and lost nearly a year of what would have been his first year at school. And, he experienced many problems before he was fully recovered, especially when the screws holding the plate in his leg would come undone causing painful sores to erupt. He was always cheerful, running and jumping about, just the same as he'd always done before. When he finally started school, the sports master wouldn't allow Billy to take part. Mum had to go to a tribunal insisting he was to take part in all the school activities, including sports. Mum was not given to failure, or negative attitudes, she 'won the day' and Billy took part in the sports, very quickly to come first in almost everything he did!

We never did hear whether the robbers were caught, nor did Billy get any sort of compensation. It was just another headline in the papers, soon forgotten. Although, we did keep the Newspaper cuttings with pictures of Billy in his hospital bed!

1948 came after the usual wonderful Christmas and New Year celebration, especially as Billy was home. Uncle John's girlfriend Mary was still the one and only 'love of his life'...coming to the house most days; she would often play games with us.

Just before Christmas, Dad bought a big black Fiat car, spending his spare time on general maintenance, making new lining for the inside roof. It was the talk of the street, everyone crowded round to inspect it, pointing to the running boards and saying 'it looked like something James Cagney would drive!'

Times were still hard in the East End, so for us to now have a car was considered by others, a huge luxury... which of course, it was! But, as more building work came in to Oakes & Son, it was a necessity for Dad to be more mobile. That same year Uncle John celebrated his 18th birthday and was called up to do his National Service, after which he'd announced, that he would marry Mary. Dad took Mum into the West End as a treat for their Wedding anniversary, where he saw one of his comrades from No. 4 Commandos who was a Mounted Policeman. He'd been riding his horse along the road, with another policemen and somehow spotted Dad and pulled him over. Mum was furious thinking they were in trouble, but it was all a hoax so his mate would have the excuse to chat to Dad about old times. It made his day and later he and George had another of their marathon chats.

As business improved for Dad he donated money to The Commando Association to help those disabled; he received newsletters regularly. Dad and George would also go to the reunions together.

Billy continued to have regular check-ups with Mr. Hyman at the London Jewish Hospital, when I would go too. He was a lovely man, robust with a florid round face, always wore a suit and a bow tie. Finally, Billy had his last operation in 1949 when the screws were removed as they were causing periodic problems. The bone had grown around the plate so it was decided that the remainder of the plate would be removed…I was really glad that everything was fine and he wouldn't have to go to the hospital anymore, but was really sad at the thought of never seeing Mr. Hyman again. Billy never had a problem after that, his leg healed well and he still continued to beat everyone in the school sports.

Also, 1949 became the year in which we would see the seaside, for the very first time, we were off to Southend-by-the-Sea. Billy and I were called early one

Saturday morning, Granny and Mum had already prepared a picnic. Dad and Granddad loaded up the car whilst Uncle George went off to get lemonade, beers, even some sweets...we all then crammed into the Fiat.

Arriving at Southend after what seemed an endless journey of rolling countryside, villages and farms on this beautiful hot sunny day. But, before reaching Southend, we made a detour to a place called Leigh-on-Sea, to find many cockle sheds that gave off a distinctive smell of shellfish, mingled with the aroma of the salty black mud and sea air. The tide was out and the different sized boats were laid this way and that as though asleep, either lying in the little creeks left by the outgoing tides, or on the top of the muddy sandbars. Behind the sheds on the short promenade huge piles of shells were stacked.

We stopped at some of the sheds to eat jellied eels, whelks and cockles, where I couldn't help but be fascinated by the rounded twang of the Essex accents, so distinctly different from that of the East End of London.

There were lots of little alleyways and steep steps leading round the backs of small cottages and little tea shops. Although Essex is a flat county, here in this small seaside village, only a short walk up the steps took us quickly to high ground, where you looked down on the sheds and out to sea; the properties dotted everywhere with no particular uniform, each house over-looking the next as the ground rose acutely. The tiny gardens were full of beautiful plants and shrubs, hollyhocks, lavatera, creeping vines over arched gateways and hanging baskets cascading with flowers of every imaginable colour. "Daddy, where's the beach, I want to make sand castles?" Billy said.

"When we get to Southend, you can make sand castles....just be patient!" Dad replied.

I was in awe of the beauty of this place, daydreaming of going out to sea in one of the boats. Later to realise that this 'window of beauty' that I'd just peeped through had ignited a deep seated love of the sea; it's sounds, it's smells, it's power and the pull it would have on me! We left then to go on to Southend itself.

Arriving at Southend, it seemed impossible to know what to explore first, especially as everyone was excited and had different priorities. Granddad suddenly blurted out to Granny...

"Mother, do you remember when we were here last? It was 1939...we all sat on the beach, and we were even singing when Gladys was pretending to play that Clarinet! Then, those people sitting behind us on the sea wall, joined in...it was great! Yeah! And, remember those two sailors, they'd shouted across to us...'Make sure to 'ave a good time...there's going to be a War!'

They were right!

As it happened, we believed them and went absolutely mad!

Spent every penny we had....even the rent money!

Just as well really, as none of us were to know that the war would be as bad, as it ended up being! Or last as long! What did we do with that photograph we had taken, of all of us? Suppose it's at home somewhere!"

Eventually, it was agreed that we'd start at the pier, proceed along the seafront to the Kursaal, then settle on the beach. When we reached the end of the long pier, there were people fishing and others sitting on benches with picnics. Billy and I jumped for joy when we heard that we would ride the train back, not only because it

'Symmonds' family in 1939 at Southend-on-Sea...
just before the War

was a long walk, over a mile, but the thought of going on the train that had past us as we'd walked, was simply thrilling! The train trundled along leisurely with rhythmic beats of the wheels on the tracks, echoing as it travelled over the wooden structure of the pier, above the sea and finally along over the beach.

Alighting from the train in the station at the end, we continued along the promenade making a number of stops, first when spotting a 'Bangers-n-Mash' shop to inspect the prices and menu...we would eat there later. Then a couple of times at the 'Penny Arcades' then a pub stop.

When looking up at the three and four storey buildings above the shops and arcades, I was struck by the workmanship. At the roofline there was white cement corbels and dentil block cornice; dividing the buildings, tall fluted pilasters with ionic capitals. Upon reaching the Kursaal itself, I was in awe of the magnificence of the huge glass dome of the entrance, a fine example of Victorian architecture; looking similar to pictures I'd seen of London's Crystal Palace. Glistening shards of sunlight shone through the dome, throwing rainbows of colour on the floor and walls, even though it had lost some of its former splendour, over the years. I didn't dream we'd be going inside or that a place like this still even existed...believing that the bombs of the war had destroyed most of England!

It was all a glorious insight into the Victorian era, even imagining the women of that time wearing elaborate hairstyles and long corseted dresses; men in top hat and tails still walking around the building, a far cry from the drabness of the East End streets. Dad purchased our entrance tickets and we went through the turnstile to enter a world of magic and wonderment!

"Oh! Look Sis'...! Billy exclaimed.

There were stalls and sideshows, firing ranges, fortune tellers, rides, a tower with a slide from the top, circling down and round it on a coconut mat...even a ghost train! Every possible delight we'd never seen anything like it before...lights flashing and music...then we came to a big glass case which, when you put money in the drawer and pushed it into the slot, the dummy policeman sat inside began to laugh, whilst moving from side to side!

It was time to go on the beach, but before arriving the grown-ups made another pub stop, the large building with many tables and chairs outside, called 'Cockney's Pride!

Daddy rarely drank alcohol, but today he had a bitter shandy! Granddad and Uncle George had a pint of brown Ale, Gran' and Mum ordered their favourite, port and lemon. Billy and I had 'fizzy orange' and a bag of crisps, inside the packet was a little twisted blue paper, pocket of salt.

Finally, we got onto the beach rushing straight down to the water's edge, throwing off our shoes and socks on the way to paddle, whilst everyone else sorted out deckchairs, towels and the picnic hamper. By the time we'd splashed about, getting all our clothes soaked, giggling and throwing the sea water in the air, everyone had settled themselves in the deckchairs. Uncle pulled out the biggest bottle of 'pop' we'd ever seen, the chunky moulded glass had a big ceramic stopper, with a rubber washer, the wire around the bottle neck secured the stopper by running through a hole in the top. When he opened it, the bubbles shot up, cascading out everywhere, the stopper clinking against the side of the bottle by its wire hinge...we all laughed!

Billy and I took our clothes off and Mum decided it was time to record the day on the 'Box Brownie' camera... lots of posing and saying 'cheese!' Billy started to make sand castles, Dad helped him...I investigated the sea-life, crabs, starfish, even finding hard white cuttlefish and shells to take home. It was hard to believe we'd already done so much that day, and it was still early afternoon... 'lots more time to do things' I thought! But, looking at some of the grown-ups relaxing after eating sandwiches and home-made pickles...they all seemed far too sleepy to play ball with us!

We carried on digging holes in the sand, making friends with some other children playing nearby. Before we knew it was time for us to go off and eat at the 'Bangers-n-Mash' shop!

Although we were hungry by then, we didn't want to leave the beach...

"Oh! Please Daddy, can we come back for a while after we've eaten, just a little while, please...?"

Secretly, I'm sure everyone felt the same way about leaving the beach, after we'd eaten we returned to our spot on the beach, finding the deckchairs still there. We stayed 'til finally the day turned to dusk, when the arcades and shops along the promenade were a dazzling blaze of coloured shimmering lights. The pier stretching out through the pitch black sea, lit by hanging bulbs looped from poles all the way to the end, creating eerie glints of colour on the waves below...the train could be seen, travelling slowly along it, the people seemed like dots in the windows!.

It was very late when we left for home, the end of the best day ever. We turned to look through the back window of the car as we left, until eventually the bright lights disappeared. Billy dropped off to sleep first...then I felt my eyelids heavier and heavier...

Chapter Twelve

We talked endlessly about our trip to Southend... telling everyone about it, and about the 'Rock Candy!' Billy...in amazement, discovered that the stick of rock we'd each been bought, had 'Southend-on-Sea' written all the way through it! We'd checked as we ate them, keeping small pieces as mementos in our bedrooms! These bits of rock eventually dissolved into a horrid mass of pink and white sticky matter that ran everywhere! We were still talking about Southend at Christmas!

It was now the New Year of 1950, a fresh new decade with the promise of better things to come, but during the run up to my 10th birthday, the following year, I became very ill. In the summer of 1950, Dad bought a large house in Stanley Avenue, Gidea Park in Essex, apparently a very sought after and expensive area...the house was very grand, certainly impressive. But, although excited about the prospect of living there, was deeply distressed at the thought of leaving Granny, Granddad and the rest of the family...it seemed so far away!

I became tired, uninterested in anything...lacking energy or enthusiasm...then I had a fall on my hip, which thereafter caused me to limp, becoming progressively worse 'til my right foot turned inward. Having always previously been an active child...Mum and Dad were concerned. Dad called Mr. Hyman, an appointment was arranged...blood was taken and other tests were done. Firstly, the tests revealed that I had Anemia quite badly, but no real explanation for the problems with my hip and leg, now significantly shorter than the other.

I was very pleased to see Mr. Hyman he kept making little jokes with me and said...

"Well it's your turn to come and stay at the London Jewish...it seems you all can't keep away! We'll soon have your better!"

By the time of my admission to Hospital I was unable to walk at all, secretly feeling extremely frightened. I was put in an isolation ward at first my right leg put in heavily weighted 'traction'...there seemed to be pulleys and equipment everywhere. I completely understood how Billy must have felt, and told him when Mum next brought him to see me.

"Well Sis', I was much younger in any case...it wasn't so bad. All the nurses played games with me...it's not quite the same for you!" he remarked.

"At least you can listen to the radio...here's some books, and look I've drawn you some pictures!"

I was in hospital for months, through Christmas and New Year, becoming increasingly fascinated with the news, listening to the broadcasts as often as possible. I'd asked Mum and Dad if I could have a Diary, with at least a page for each day, and got one for Christmas. I would start my entries about my day's activities, but most importantly I would record important events, from radio news broadcasts. If I was bored, I would sit in bed and mimic the voices...BBC radio voices were precise, very much spoken to a standard expected by Royalty, in only acceptably clear posh tones! The 'news bulletins' could only be read by men with 'consistent' pronunciation and professional performance. "Shall I do my BBC voice, Mum...listen!" Sounding like Princes Elizabeth as I spoke with everyone suitably amused!

It was 28th January the news broadcast came on...the newsreader saying: Navada Desert rocked by Nuclear Tests. I listened intently, as he spoke. Wind rushed through the streets of Las Vegas and the residents of Boulder City reported rooms lit up by a flash of light as the US Atomic Energy Commission exploded the second of two nuclear bombs in as many days, in the Nevada Desert. Las Vegas lay 45 miles from the boundary of the test grounds, while Boulder City was 100 miles from the explosion site. Keen to allay the natural fears of people in the region, the Atomic Energy Commission issued a statement saying, patrols found 'no indication of any radiological hazards' after the tests. Although, all civil aircraft flights within a 150-mile radius of the site was to be grounded. 'Wow! This is very important, better put is in my diary!' I thought...writing it all down immediately.

Various recorded entries each day included my Birthday on 8th February, 1951 where I wrote: 'It's my birthday today...I am 10 years old, a very important birthday. I wish I'd been celebrating 'it' today at home, but I'm still not better, and Mr. Hyman says that he still doesn't know exactly what's wrong with me, but it's something to do with my blood! He gave me a present too...a really special pen. I will keep it forever and from now on I will use it to write my diary. Can't wait to see everyone later, especially Billy...I want him to tell me all the news from School. I shall write some more later, when it's the end of the day!' I'll put the diary under the pillow 'til then.

Being unable to walk about, play with other children and go to school contributed to my already 'older than my years' attitudes and 'old fashioned' manner. I also discovered a preference for being around and talking to adults, rather than my own age group.

30th March, 1951...I recorded in my Diary. 'Today I heard a news report, saying: 'New Spy Fever as Rosenbergs Convicted'. Then I saw the newspaper...'As Western Countries experienced the Red Menace first-hand in Korea and rumour-mills still churned over the espionage convictions of Alger Hiss and Klaus Fuchs in 1950, New Yorkers Julius and Ethal Rosenberg couldn't have faced spying charges at a worse time. Their three week trial ended today with 32 year old Julius, an Army Signal Corps engineer, and his wife 35 year old Ethel being pronounced 'guilty' of passing US Atomic secrets to the Russians at the end of WWII.

Later, the Rosenbergs who protested their innocence throughout their Trial were sentenced to death by Judge Irving R. Kaufman on 5th April, being finally sent to the electric chair on 19th June, 1953. Now hearing talk about the 'Iron Curtain' of the 'Cold War' which had descended; did fill me with questions!

Spies, espionage, MI5 and whispers of the threat of the Cold War and Communism...it felt as though we'd been weaned on stuff like 'walls have ears'...'loose lips, sink ships'...living always with a veil of secrecy, invisibly around us. I became increasingly interested in learning about the Reds and espionage, looking and listening for news stories. I suppose plenty of people were also interested...hence stories of Dick Barton, Special Agent on the BBC's Light Programme.

4th May, 1951...I wrote: 'Today I heard the most exciting thing on the radio...King George VI and Queen Elizabeth officially opened The Festival of Britain. I will ask Mummy and Daddy today, when they visit me, whether they will take Billy and me to see it. Shall will myself to get better...I must get better before the Festival ends in September. Mr. Hyman says it cost over £8 Million to build. When he came to see me today, he told me I'm going to have a plaster cast put on the whole of my leg and more blood tests and different medication. He says he will let me have a special magazine about the Festival, to read and report information in my diary. He is so kind to me, but I wish he would tell me soon that I can go home...it's been nearly 7 months now in hospital, at least I think it is. I'm sure that Mr. Hyman knows what's wrong with me, but I'm probably not allowed to know!

Daddy has found someone to rent the house in Gidea Park, a Director of Marconi...sounds very important! He has a wife and three children and they have signed a rental agreement, for a year. I am so glad because that will bring some money in, also it means we will not be moving from Gran's for at least a year...Yippee!

Mr Hyman has just been again today and brought me the magazine about the Festival. He said that I'm clever to read such grown up books and magazines. The article says lots about the festival, things like, it includes a new, ultra-modern stylish concert and classical music venue, The Festival Hall. It features a host of new inventions and designs under a vast construction known as The Dome of Discovery. The 27 acre site on the south bank of the Thames transformed a derelict bomb site into a kaleidoscope of light with a funfair, riverside walkways and a fun railway. The article also said that the Festival of Britain allowed a nation, still beset by post-war austerity, fuel shortages, food rationing and international strife, to let their hair down and catch a glimpse of how the future might look. Dominating the site, apparently suspended in mid-air, the neon-lit futuristic shape of The Skylon, loomed like a giant aluminium exclamation mark. The whole thing was planned to coincide with the 100th Anniversary of Prince Albert's Great Exhibition in 1851. When it finishes in September only The Festival Hall will be left as a lasting memory.'

12th May, 1951....'I'm writing my diary today, as I am very excited that Daddy has promised, if I get better before the Festival finishes in September, he will take us all! I told him, that I'd made up my mind to be better by

Festival of Britain Street Party Celebration – 1951

THE ASHES OF NASS BEACON

then...so I will! I did get to go to the Festival and also to Auntie's Street Party...

But, on a sad note...the radio said today that there had been H-Bomb tests: The Tiny Pacific Coral Island of Eniwetok was the scene of the first Hydrogen bomb test carried out today by the US Atomic Commission and Department of Defense. Although an official statement was light on details, the Commission said the test had exceeded expectations. The Hydrogen Bomb will be a hundreds of times more powerful than the Atomic bombs which destroyed Hiroshima and Nagasaki in 1945. This successful test indicates a strong US lead in the nuclear field and signals a new and more hectic round of international arms race as Russian Scientists set about creating their own destructive devices.'

7th June, 1951...not only was I returned in hospital but I heard the sad news today that the King is sick, I hope he's better soon and he's not in hospital too long! Princess Elizabeth will stand in for the King at the Trooping of the Colour ceremony, in London today. I wish I could see it. One day perhaps we will have one of those Televisions that everyone's talking about. Billy said there's a new shop opened in Burdett Road and when they went to have 'Pie-n-Mash' they went along to the shop afterwards to look at them. They even had them switched on in the window, with a big sign saying...T.V. Rental per week! Billy said people were pushing and shoving to look! There's other stuff in the news today, about spies, headlines:

'International Hunt for Burgess and MacLean'

Two weeks after they mysteriously vanished from London, British Diplomats Guy Burgess and Donald

MacLean officially became the subject of an international hunt, when the British government asked police in Britain, France, Austria and Germany to help locate and apprehend them. The security implications of their disappearance were serious. Both had served in sensitive Washington posts. MacLean (38) was First Secretary in the British Embassy, before returning to London to become head of the American Department of the Foreign Office. Burgess (40) was Second Secretary in Washington for eight months before having a nervous breakdown. While official sources in London were still being coy about the possible 'double defection' to the Soviet Union and would only confirm that both had been suspended for being 'absent without leave' the US newspapers openly voiced suspicions and official concerns with Soviet links. This is so exciting, I must show Billy this story and I'll tell Mr. Hyman too. He said this morning that we was going to buy his wife, her very own car, but will probably wait 'til the beginning of August. It's something to do with the new 'number plates'... not quite sure what he meant!'

1st August, 1951...'Today I feel much better, although my legs are still weak, mainly the right one. I have to go home soon, I simply must...perhaps they will let me out in a wheelchair...I will ask! Mr. Hyman hasn't come this morning, perhaps he's gone to look at cars? I heard them on the radio that the prices were going up especially the Austin A40 which is apparently the UK's bestselling family saloon. I bet that's what Mr. Hyman will buy his wife because they have children...it will be good for shopping and picnics. They cost a great deal of money though, £685.10 shillings for a new one'.

2nd August, 1951...'Mr. Hyman came today...I told him that I was becoming very sad, and felt very distant from Mum, Dad and Billy. I had to admit to crying when I told him, that I thought if I didn't go home soon...I would stay here forever. He says he will see what he can do! Then he said that his wife was pleased with her car, he'd purchased a new Austin A40!'

10th August, 1951...'This day is the best for a long time. Mummy and Daddy came today, they'd had a meeting with the Consultant, Mr. Hyman who has agreed to let me come home. I'll still have to rest and not become too stressed! He has made a special arrangement for me to use a hospital wheel-chair, until I'm able to walk properly by myself again. Yippee! I'm so happy, going home tomorrow!'

11th August, 1951...'I had breakfast...all the nurses came to wish me luck, some gave me little gifts. I will miss everyone, but looking forward to going home to 7 Cantrell Road. Dad will be here soon, shall pack my things now....

12th August, 1951...'It's really wonderful to be home again, everyone came to visit when I got back yesterday. Busy, busy all day long...feeling a bit like royalty. I had to be carried to bed and of course carried down again, but I've a special place made for me, near the kitchenette range. This is fantastic because I can see everything that goes on...the chats, the visitors, preparing food and cooking it. Also I can listen to the radio and still write my diary. I'm even going again to the Festival of Britain with Billy. He says, he wants to push me in the wheelchair! 'Tug' called as well last night, he brought some Herrings, caught fresh that day. Gran' has cleaned them and laid them in her special vinegar recipe she calls 'Soused

Herrings' cooked in the oven, with other spices. Delicious, great with bread and butter!

Uncle George says he wants to rent a television, mainly for Gran' and Granddad, but it will keep me entertained as well. I would be jumping in the air, if I could...but Billy did the jumping for both of us'.

15th August, 1951...'I write something every day in this diary, but some days have more important news than others. Today is an important 'diary day' because we have just had the rental T.V. delivered and had a special aerial fitted. It's a very small, fuzzy 'black and white' picture, taking a long time before the man fitting the aerial could get the picture clear! The excitement soon faded as there didn't seem to be much on it to watch. Gran' said she preferred the radio!'

24th August, 1951...'I'm writing in my diary today, because I've just heard about more sinister news. I thought somehow, when the war was over that we would feel safe and secure, hearing good things. It seems, everywhere you look there's bad news, sometimes frightening or vengeful news. Today's radio news broadcast said:

'Mau Mau influence spreads...Kenyan police today publicly linked a series of burglaries in the white suburbs of the capital Nairobi to the secret political society called Mau Mau, and admitted a growth in its influence among black Africans seeking independence from Britain. Authorities have been aware of the sinister Mau Mau's existence for about a year and only know that oaths to drive the white man from Kenya are sworn by Kikuyu tribe recruits, attending secret meetings in the forest outside Nairobi'.

23rd September, 1951...'Oh! It's so sad our King is very ill. The radio newsreader said: '*Major Lung operation for King George.*

A huge crowd gathered anxiously outside the gates of Buckingham Palace in London this afternoon, awaiting official word of the condition of King George, who underwent two-hour surgery to remove his left lung yesterday'.

The bulletin, signed by the King's eight doctors, was finally posted in a picture frame by a palace official who carried it to the main gate, accompanied by two policemen. Newsmen from around the world pressed forward to photograph the inch and a half high black crayoned letters announcing the King's condition as 'as satisfactory as could be expected'. Doctors had diagnosed a lung disease on 8th September, but news of this was kept quiet while treatment options were reviewed and the eventual decision to operate was taken. While Prime Minister Clement Attlee, who'd called an October General Election only 4 days earlier, cut short a brief holiday in North Berwick to return to London. A private service for the King's recovery was held at the Chapel of Lambeth Palace, London by the Archbishop of Canterbury, Dr. Geoffrey Fisher'.

26th October, 1951...'The news is full of the General Election...'Churchill' back at Number 10 Downing Street. With the information in the paper saying: Stung and hurt by the electorate's rejection of him in 1945 when he assumed Britain's voters would naturally keep their wartime leader as the nation's first post-war Prime Minister, Winston Churchill returned to power today as his Conservative Party won a narrow victory over Clement Attlee's divided Labour Party. Now aged 77, Churchill left Buckingham Palace after accepting his commission from King George. Apparently recovering well from his major surgery last month, to say he relished the chance to revitalise Britain's fortunes by freeing the country from Labour's socialist ideal and alleged mis-management. Remarkably, this Warlord who'd been photographed with two other titans, Roosevelt and Stalin at Yalta in 1945, their rivalry and petty prejudices were evident. Churchill would now have the last laugh he was back in Downing Street as Britain's Prime Minister. Hitler and Roosevelt were dead and by 1953, Stalin would be dead too. By then Churchill nearly 80 years, the only Warlord who'd survived!'

27th October, 1951...'Suez is periodically source for news reports, but although I want to report in my diary, the full details and items of real importance, today I think I will just help with the Christmas preparations. We will start making the Christmas Puddings today, and the mustard pickle, red cabbage and pickled onions. I will write all about Suez another time....it seems very complicated. I think I will have to ask Dad or Grandfather what it's about, and then make some notes!.

Chapter Thirteen

Sometimes, during the winter months we would have thick fog in fact it was more appropriately called 'smog!' The early months of 1952 were no exception. One particular day when Mum came to meet us from school, she couldn't see us coming out of the gate, nor could we see her...even though only feet away; the smog was so thick like 'pea-soup' we'd all say! Fortunately, we heard her calling and finally found each other. It's a strange and eerie thing, to stretch out your arm and be unable to see your hand, or any defining line...it made you feel compelled to check it was there by touching and feeling every finger, with the other invisible hand. The strange thing about doing this was...although you knew you were checking and feeling your own hand, the brain played tricks...there was the sensation momentarily of touching someone else's hand, instantaneously intermingled with the sense, you'd been grabbed by another person! We are told 'Smokeless Fuel' will eventually end these smog's...we'll see!

The problems with my bones improved and by the Summer I was walking with relative ease, some days would be better than others, when I would need walking sticks...being back at school was great! Many things were changing...Uncle John and Mary married, later than originally planned; they'd waited to give me chance to get better as I was to be a bridesmaid, Billy a pageboy. It was a fantastic day, the sun shone bright, and I could hear the Holy Trinity Church bells pealing. The congregation of friends and family seemed enormous; our neighbours were there too...it was a wonderful wedding and a fantastic party in true 'Symmonds' style! They went off on a honeymoon...for a week, after which they would move into their flat next door at No. 6 Cantrell Road. They had the whole top section of the house belonging to Mr. Keale. Uncle John and Mary, officially now our Aunt, worked really hard before they got married decorating their flat. They have all the latest 'mod-cons' ...and they always have instant coffee...Nescafe 37 as well as tea! They have the latest Formica table and matching tubular chairs...all their furniture and décor, is in bright colours. There's a clock on the wall with different sized spikes of brass and black...it looks like the 'Sun...with its rays!' They even have a vacuum cleaner...it's magic...and they're going to buy a Dansette record player, for the new 45rpm records, which also plays the 78's.

They still have their wind-up gramophone...which sometimes slows down, right in the middle of the music! They both wear really fashionable clothes...'Oh! How I wished I was already a grown-up...times are really exciting. I'd love to have my own place too....and modern things!'

"Still daydreaming I see". Mummy said...

"C'mon, we've things to do...!"

We watched television a bit more now, especially when later ITV began broadcasting, more to see and a choice with commercial T.V. Newsreel footage really does produce impact to what's being reported, but I still like to listen to the radio. Sometimes though, I have thought to myself...'News is always...bad, why can't they report nice things occasionally?'

The 1950's has seen reports of events like...floods in North Devon, taking 36 lives in Lynmouth, while a plane at the Farnborough Air Show broke the sound barrier, but then crashed killing 26 spectators.

Since the end of the War depression or mental sickness was causing some people to do unimaginable things. I remember sitting on the front step, after it had been freshly cleaned with whitener in the mornings, and watching the beautiful, slim, red haired Vivien from No. 9 Cantrell Road, pass the house on her way to work. She always walked very elegantly and I would think to myself how much I would like to look as nice as her, when I grew older. I remember the first time I saw her with her boyfriend...they looked so attentive to each other; they got engaged and later married. I remember too, some years before-hand...seeing Joyce Keale coming out of the next door house, where Uncle John and Aunt Mary now live. She would sometimes be with her daughter, Mary and her little granddaughter, Evelyn. I remember the shock waves through our house after we'd heard that Joyce had gone out one morning and never returned. She'd gone to the 'Stink House Bridge' over the Limehouse Cut, taken off her wedding ring, folded her coat, laid her hat and scarf on the top; in full view of people looking out of the factory windows, she jumped from the bridge into the 'filthy, putrid waters' below and drowned herself! Nobody knew why? Soon after the funeral, Mary and little Evelyn disappeared...again, nobody knew why, there were rumours and whispers for a while, then no further word...just gone!

I constantly puzzled at life and people, thinking often about the driving mechanics of man...why are humans so wicked and destructive. Throughout my childhood I'd find myself studying my parents and grandparents, when they were in repose and peaceful, dosing in their chairs or going about simple everyday jobs together. Secretly, I'd try to figure out what passed between man and woman that invisibly was the thing, they called 'love'...they'd argue sometimes, then the next moment they'd laugh...moments of flame and passion? But I felt 'love' was rather like 'religion' something indefinable, there seemed no suitable dictionary meaning, or explanation, certainly not by any normal mode of language, I understood! Hearing those baffling phrases like 'you'll know when it happens!' and 'when you're older you'll understand! Why is it such a mystery?

I later realised that 'nobody seems to know how to explain what 'love' is'...so I tried to work it out! Was it sinister or benevolent, tender or explosive...these electric charges of passion I sense at times! How would these forces play their part when I come to feel this mystery emotion, for this unknown man that's yet to enter my life! I thought about this imponderable event, with both pleasure and terror! Guess I was entering troubled adolescence!

Although my security and happiness was founded in 7 Cantrell Road, Bow...where the house retained the flavour of both kindergarten and sanctuary; the recent changes caused me to question my whole understanding of security.

As time passed I began to feel free again from the worries of 'how people ticked'...and the torment of questions like 'would I suddenly want to do strange things or develop a strange mind?' Then, just as these worries were subsiding, my world was turned up-side-down again. The adored and envied, elegantly beautiful Vivien...who I so wanted to be like when I got older... did something terrible, beyond belief!

She'd been married about a year and worked at the big Yardeley factory near Stratford; rumour has it that she was expecting a baby, so why wasn't she happy? She said goodbye to her husband and family, then left home as usual, arrived on the Mile End Underground Station and as a train came in to the platform she threw herself onto the rails, in front of it...she didn't stand a chance! I sobbed and sobbed. The rest of the year was reasonably happy, but always tinged with sadness at the memory of Vivien.

The continued illness of the King, finally gave way to his sad demise and on the 2nd June, 1953 was the Coronation of Elizabeth, as Queen of England. Not only was it on the television, but we had another street party...it was great! It was another marvellous excuse for the release of my many butterflies, that's what I called my daydreams they were my 'butterflies'...techni-coloured wonderment! It's so exciting...

"We're Elizabethan's now!" I declared...

"We've got a new glamorous, young Queen... it's a new Elizabethan era!"

Billy scoffed! "Sissy, you get more silly, every day!"

On my journey towards adulthood, I gradually realised that in this new period of prosperity with cars, coffee bars and skiffle groups, I was now 'one' of a new age era...which the advertisers had invented. I would be a teenager in a time when it was considered, we're the real inheritors of the 'You've Never Had It So Good' society, immortalised into a slogan by Prime Minister Harold Macmillan. It seemed we had it all: our own film heroes, James Dean and Marlon Brando, our own fashions...our own radio comics in The Goon Show, performing a weekly lampooning of all that was 'pompous' in authority!

As years turned from one to the next, even our Christmas presents were beyond belief. Billy got a Meccano set...and he made a face with it like the Mekon in the Eagle...it looked quite terrifying!

I'd got a 'Teddy Bear'...it really did look like a bear, and when you turned it on its back, then turned it forward, it would make a groaning sound! I also got a Bunty book, at the back of which was cut-out dolls, and cut-out clothes. Mum had a Twink Home Perm and a new 'with it' hairdo...I'm not sure though whether Dad was impressed!

I remember the early television programmes with great affection, especially Granny's favourite, Emergency Ward 10...set in Oxbridge General Hospital with upbeat storylines, a medical soap...concentrating on the lives and loves of the staff! Mum liked this programme too! Mum and Dad used to like to listen to Hancock's Half Hour on the radio, it was a massively popular sitcom. We'd listen to it, eating streaky bacon sandwiches, slices of freshly baked Bloomer loaf...bacon and lashings of Daddy's Brown Sauce.

Billy and I would often listen to this programme as well. When Hancock was put on the T.V., it was still very popular...it started with the 'tuba signature tune' and the breathless announcement of 'H-H-Hancock's Half Hour...with Sid James as the cynical room-mate.

There was so many good programmes 'The Adventures of Robin Hood' - 'Dixon of Dock Green' - 'I Love Lucy' - 'The Lone Ranger'...Billy, loved this programme. He now insisted on being called Bill Jnr., especially as he wore long trousers, which were held up by the really snappy new style of belt...it was elasticated with coloured stripes in red and green, with a 'snake' clip to fasten it! But, despite the adult title of Bill Jnr., he still enjoyed leaping around with a cry of 'Hi-Ho-Silver' pretending to ride off to the strains of the William Tell Overture... righting wrongs and punishing the baddies!

Bill played outside in the street or over the cemetery with his friends. One of them would be Tonto, the trusty Indian sidekick of the Lone Ranger, with the others being the baddies. I often wanted to play as well, but boringly girls weren't allowed...

"It's not fair!" I'd moan, but it made no difference... quite amusing really, signs of prejudice, even then!

I really believed then... that it was really 'dull' being a girl, boys seemed to have so much more fun! The other games that the boys played were Davy Crockett, Rawhide or Ivanhoe and sometimes 'Robin Hood'.

Andy Pandy was the king of children's television...the leader of the 'Watch with Mother' pack of Rag Tag and Bobtail, the Flower Pot Men and the Wooden Tops...also Blue Peter. The game shows were good called Double Your Money, Take Your Pick...also the programme detailing people lives in This Is Your Life compared by Aamon Andrews. But, many things were changing...

The barrel arches under the railway at the back, where people had taken refuge during the bombing had been turned into little businesses. There was a Wine Merchants, a Mechanic, repairing cars and motorbikes, a Carpenter and all sorts of other small merchants. On the corner of Cantrell Road where the first three houses had been bombed, had been cleared, but instead of new houses being built...the ground was fenced off and a huge Alsatian dog was kept in there on a long chain. It would bark ferociously when you went past the gates. I'm not sure what went on in the yard, but green lorries would go in and out!

Then further up the street where the other houses had been bombed, from No. 12 onwards...the ground was also cleared. Then pre-fabricated single storey houses were built which every called 'pre-fabs'. They were square temporary homes with a little garden...dotted about on the area where the old houses used to be. They looked really out of place, but served the purpose of providing much needed accommodation. They were quick to erect and inexpensive in comparison to brick built homes, being made of pre-formed sections that slotted together, with flat roofs. A girl called Maria and her family moved into one of the pre-fabs...was glad to make a new friend, but not so glad about the other changes in the street. Especially when I heard that my best friend Janet Towler, would be moving.

We hugged each other with tears rolling down our faces...Janet finally got into the removal lorry to take the long journey to Thetford, Norfolk. It may as well been the end of the world, as far as I was concerned, in fact, I thought Norfolk was the end of the world! I missed her so much when she left...then a few months later, the 'Commons' family announced that they were emigrate to Australia...a real blow. Granma' and Grandpa' were very emotional on the day they left, everyone was, including Mum and Dad...they had been such extraordinary neighbours and characters in their own right! Granma' made some jokes about how they'd get on in Australia...but every word she spoke was mixed sounds of laughter and of choking back tears!

"Ada will be running the Country before the year's out...you mark my words!" Gran' declared!

A family called 'Evans' moved in.

"They seem well-off, Bill!"

"How d'ya know, Sis?"....

"I don't, but they have a 'Jaguar XK140 Coupe... that's got to be a pretty penny...their furniture's posh looking too! Really up-to-date stuff!"

"Bill...I really hope 'Tug' doesn't decide to take a move to one of those 'new towns' like Harlow or Dagenham...he says, he's going to take me on his boat, fishing at sea and stuff!"

"Your weird Sissy, girls aren't supposed to like going on boats and sea fishing!"

But it was something I wanted to do...I just loved to be in, or on the water. I loved the smell of the boats, the sea, the fish...everything! True to his word we went fishing, out at Sea. Granddad was there too, he often went out fishing with 'Tug'...we brought back some herring and skate. We often went out fishing after that, it was great...I was only a bit sea sick on the first trip, but fine after that.

One day 'Tug' announced...

"My nephew's coming to stay for a while, I'll introduce him to you, George, when he gets here"...

"His name's Willie...Willie Flynn!"

I took little notice!

Although I loved to go out with the boys, fishing and doing boy's stuff...there was still an opposite extreme to my character, an alter-ego, the opposite end of my personality scale that liked the 'ladylike' refined luxuries of life! I'd made up my mind that one day I would be wealthy although, I hadn't even decided what sort of work I would do! I had already left school at Christmas, and would be 15 years old on 8th February, 1956.

By chance I'd seen an advertisement in the newspaper, saying 'GPO Telephonists Wanted' details on application... I decided to apply.

It was unlikely we'd move just yet as Dad had continued to rent out the house at Gidea Park, Essex so, if I succeeded in getting in to the G.P.O. I would be able to complete the training. The more I thought about it, the more enthusiastic I was about becoming a telephonist as it was really considered a 'good job' and well paid too. I sensed some unspoken reservations within the family, probably because in those days the emphasis on speech, was absolute 'Queens English' required, but luckily I had an ability to mimic...

"I can speak very la-di-da...when I want" I informed everyone.

I went off to take the interview at the Telephonist Recruitment Centre in Holborn, London determined to get accepted. I had various tests to take, spelling, grammar, a speech test which involved wearing apparatus and answering questions speaking through the 'head-set!' It was, I have to admit, quite daunting especially remembering to speak always perfect English. I constantly heard Grans' voice in my head saying 'Remember your P's and Q's....and you'll be alright!'

The interview tests seemed to take forever, but it took around an hour after which time I was told by one of the officious gentlemen interviewers, that I would hear in due course. A period of around a week or so, of torture before the letter came to announce their decision. Wondering whether I would I be saying 'Operator… What is your number please?'…speaking at the end of the telephone line, or not? The letter finally arrived…I was in. I jumped around the kitchenette, waving the letter in the air, which detailed where I was to go, the date of my start and so on.

"I've got the job…I've been accepted! I screamed.

Also, the job offer letter contained information about the fact that as a 'GPO Telephonist' I would be required to sign 'The Official Secrets Act'…this made the job seem all the more important. In fact it was much later that I realised just how much sensitive information 'one' was privy to as a 'telephonist' in those days, every call then had to be directed through a telephonist. Whether a 'call-box' or Parliament, the Royal Mint or the Port of London, Scotland Yard, the Foreign Office or MI5. We connected the call, and we could listen in!

This was a time of great activity in MI5 collecting human-source intelligence and I heard the name 'Ustinov'many times, mentioned in calls. Hearing his voice when calls were connected his 'phone at his flat in Kensington. Discussing on one occasion his journey into Holland to lead Wolfgang zu Putlitz out to safety, after he'd decided to defect in 1940. Ustinov had been recruited by MI5 obtaining high-grade intelligence about the state of German rearmament, priceless pre-war intelligence.

Talks went on about the Communist Party of Great Britain, especially links with the trade union movement, conversations of the post-war K.G.B. activities. The name 'Ustinov' of course, struck a chord but, many of the conversations I would pick up on had no real relevance at the time. Later, my curiosity to anything remotely connected with espionage or the 'Cold War' I connected the name 'Ustinov' and realised that Klop Ustinov was the father of Peter Ustinov, the actor.

One afternoon whilst I was on 'switch room duty' one of the calls connected was a call for help. An MI6 training operation had apparently gone wrong, having to make a call for help. An MI6 search party had gone in to a block of flats to head for their training target, to locate and interrogate. They'd mis-counted the floors, proceeding to pick the lock of a flat, one floor above the correct floor. They'd then grabbed the man inside, going to work on him, whilst he protested his innocence... continuing their interrogation believing his actions to be part of the ruse! The over-enthusiastic trainee search party continued, with true textbook 'persuasion' tactics and eventually had him naked as a jay-bird and singing just as well...they'd in fact captured a jewel thief, who'd pulled off a diamond heist.

Not only did they have him singing like a 'canary' but he produced the 'loot' which was still in his possession, the robber believing he'd been captured by a rival 'underworld' gang!

Colleagues and I were laughing, although we couldn't share the story...nor, did I understand the implications or the sensitive nature of the information passed in those calls. But, it later had relevance when the story broke of Burgess and MacLean who defected in 1951 and remembering references often made in those calls, to the mystery 'third man!' Many years later in 1979 the wartime MI5 officer, art historian and former Surveyor of the Queen's pictures, Sir Anthony Blunt...finally disclosed that he was a Russian Spy!

I smiled as I thought to myself one day...'working at the G.P.O. is a great life, if you can stand the excitement!' At least I was no longer in personal misery, my co-workers actually spoke to me now, after the early weeks of being sent to Coventry...by day, I speak perfect English in my posh 'telephone voice'...by night, a 'cockney sparrow!'

After a while I became dissatisfied with the job, I wanted more or just maybe different. I think I'll try my hand at having a market stall...I'll sell clothes! Girls always want new clothes...I'll start with a stall on the market, at weekends then I'll save and buy a shop. Yes, that's what I'll do!

Chapter Fourteen

Willie finally came to stay with 'Tug' in the Spring of 1957. I'd just turned 16 years old, but actually looked older, or so I'm told. Willie Flynn was 19 years old...cutting a fine dash of a man at 6ft. 4ins., and ruggedly handsome. His hair long for that time fell about his face in thick tousled waves. His voice was deep, gravelly and confidently seductive. He was a perfect 'walking cliché' of predatory male sexuality...with dancing eyebrows that mocked as he spoke and a flashing Cheshire cat smile, a seemingly brazen Lothario that secretly feared the opposite sex...later admitting his sense of failure with woman, due to his tendency to date tough, strong-willed, uncompromising women and felt a 'victim' when they left. But, in truth he drove his women away! He held a deep rooted mistrust of womankind beginning as lovers, he'd turn them all into sisters and friends, with a cynical view of relations between the sexes, he'd say...

"You women hate us, force us to tell lies...and you don't play fair!"

His arms were 'powerful' his legs gorgeous, well formed from manual work on his Father's boat, his chiseled good looks irresistible to most women he met!

'I'm safe...he's not my type!' I'd thought feeling smug, whilst...gradually being drawn into an invisible vortex, by his unfailing charisma.

His incredible female following especially from his part time work as a DJ earned him a title in the 'café society' of *'stud du jour'* his sharp wit finely honed, intelligently delivered, was capable of stripping bare a person's weaknesses, with one swift blow.

We eventually embarked on a powerful relationship whilst both pursuing our independent dreams...with me travelling to visit him on Mersea Island, other times he would visit me in the East End. Emotionally, both on a 'quest for the impossible'...discovering, we both had issues and strange 'shadow' aspects that secretly would drive us! Our relationship at close quarters would be doomed! Both of us the kind of people it seemed, others broke themselves on. Together our love was 'white hot' with a raging passion for each other burning bright... both to excite and destroy; neither of us knew how to deal with these emotions!

We'd rented a flat together against our respective families' wishes as 'living together' was still frowned upon; but as we planned to marry, reluctantly our parents gave us their blessing!

But, we parted acrimoniously, before our wedding day and before we were totally destroyed each other. It would be some years before we would come full circle to realise and accept our inter-dependency. No matter what wars we'd fought in the past we needed each other, becoming inseparable! But we travelled many a road before this happened...

Determined to get a car and open my first shop by the latest 1960...I would at least get started with a market stall in my spare time. Later, I sold dresses full time, giving up my job as a GPO Telephonist. I'd found some small factories to cut and machine my own designs, also some shop outlets who would buy from me wholesale. I bought my first car in 1959, a Ford Anglia, it all seemed so wonderful!

Somehow, I still wanted something more, better fashions, better quality, always searching...

"I think I'll go and have a look at the Paris Fashions!" I announced.

Willie and I decided to live together again and were looking for a flat, when suddenly I had a brilliant idea...

"I want to get a shop, we want to get a flat...let's do both!"

Off we both went to see what was on the market. Everything in our lives was...go! go! go! We found a shop in Romford it was the best compromise all round, it was near to Gidea Park, Mum and Dad had finally moved there to live. It was affordable, it had a large flat over and it was still within driving distance for Willie to get to his boatshed on Mersea Island. I could also get to visit and stay with Gran and Granddad, whilst our visits could coincide with seeing Willie's uncle 'Tug'.

Seemed too good to be true, perhaps that's exactly what it was?

Maybe, we were too ambitious...

The shop was up and running, we'd settled into the flat...opening a bottle of champagne to celebrate, whilst I examined my *'piece de resistance'* the certificate showing my new Company 'Raffles'...just the start we agreed. The shop was opened in grand style we had a big party...publicity, the works.

A flight was booked for the following week, to go to Paris for Fashion Week. Willie would be in Mersea, finishing a boat he was building. Whilst in Paris, I was to meet Margot, it was a chance meeting...she'd helped me when Orly Airport had lost my luggage. Although I usually made few female friends, we hit it off straight away, quickly becoming close to remain friends always...she helped me find my way around Paris, speaking very good English she could translate, as my French was non-existent! What French I knew, was of little use!

She had a real eye for fashion, though she was a trained dancer. Her voice simply amazing...she was never short of work offers, and worked in a nightclub in the most fashionable part of Paris night-life. I stayed in Paris for two weeks instead of the planned one week... Willie wasn't very pleased. I suggested he came out for a break, but he said he was too busy. Margot and I travelled to places where she grew up, telling me about her life. It was obvious she had come from a wealthy background, having spent some of her schooling in England at a Girls Boarding School, but her parents, and grandparents had been killed during the War. They had been part of the 'underground' and the Germans had found out and shot them all. Margot stayed in England for as long as she could then she returned to France when it was safe, after the war.

I came home saying my goodbyes to Margot and arranged that she would come and visit as soon as possible...she would come for Christmas, I couldn't wait. Raffles was doing well, the wholesale business was too and money was coming in...soon the boat Willie was building would be finished and he could sell it!

It was really good times in fashion world with Carnaby Street in London's West End considered the epicentre of swinging London. Will and I had gathered a set of 'like-minded' friends 'a wild bunch' we'd have parties... music was fantastic, the Beatles, the Rolling Stones... fashion was Quant with Twiggy wearing mini-dresses. It's was crazy, times were crazy...even crazy too were things like the Tax Rules having to be changed in 1965! The Treasury was losing so much money over the success of the miniskirt, because they levied Tax by the length of material!

My life had become one huge 'merry-go-round'....I'd always felt, especially when I was growing up, on the edge of life, not realising I'd already stepped in, amongst the 'hedonists' of its time...it hadn't seemed difficult. In fact, Willie and I were the 'in' people that everyone wanted to be seen with and party with!

Margot and I also successfully formed a partnership, opening several shops in the UK and also in France, starting with Paris, we were making serious money. This partnership caused problems within my relationship with Willie...putting off our wedding plans, as we were spending more time apart, business demanding so much of my time.

We found ourselves unable to live without each other or be apart for too long, and the resulting jealousies often meant we couldn't live with each other, either! We'd bought a London Flat in Marloes Road near the King's Road and a small cottage on Mersea Island, which was my favourite place to relax. Wherever we managed to arrange time together we'd always end with a party...our parties now quite famous amongst the 'jet set'. Will's robust sense of humour and wicked wit and my return banter made us a 'double act' that other's enjoyed; though behind the scenes it was often emotional carnage.

I caught him in our Jacuzzi with another woman on one occasion...all hell broke loose, especially when on yet another different occasion the other woman...was Margot! "Nothing happened...what's the problem?" He'd insisted.

As far as he was concerned, the three of us should enjoy ourselves...'I should get in too...have a glass of Champagne and relax!'

When we were first together, struggling for money everything was great...our time off from work would be spent working on his boat, Sea Wolf...this boat he used as a ferry. We'd either anti-foul the bottom of the boat or spend time repainting the deck, which satisfied the simple qualities of his character. But, there was another side...dark and demanding, triggered when he abused drugs and alcohol following the excesses of success. Money was simply rolling in now, Willie had sold Sea Wolf and bought a big old yacht, and we'd spend a lot of time sailing in the stately twin-masted schooner...called 'Void Moon'. Willie was a serious and accomplished sailor, often taking the boat into stormy waters, but he always knew how to handle her.

We roamed the hotspots of St. Tropez, Cannes, Monte Carlo where we would meet with Margot, and 'Void Moon' would be crammed with party-goers, invited aboard by the now often infuriating, over-indulgent and libidinous...Willie Flynn! Finding it difficult to deal with Will's urges, often fuelled by Wild Turkey and recreational drugs, salted away in the mahogany-lined master cabin...with the worst of all times when he received more than one 'paternity suit' resulting from his wild nights. Even getting arrested after a particularly nasty incident!

On this occasion we'd been partying offshore of the Riviera with some French girlfriends of Margot's. His larger than life personality that usually dominated the party was noticeably absent! This sudden absence was a sure indication that a female was involved…discovering Willie with the girl in our cabin, I demanded that she be taken ashore.

To everyone's horror, he carried her to the side of the boat…gave her some money and a lifebelt and threw her over the side, telling her to swim ashore…yelling after her, as she landed in the water…

"See, it pays to be a good girl!"….

I was never keen on buying 'Void Moon' just the mere thought of the astrological implications gave me the creeps…

"Nothing good comes from any situation started, when the Moon becomes 'Void of Course!"

"Things just never pan out, why would anyone want a boat called 'Void Moon'…it's a cosmic catastrophe!" I'd insisted.

Will's reaction was to completely mock my views as utter rubbish, and display his complete control over his destiny!

Willie made his first act upon purchasing 'Void Moon'…to devise a new Pennant for the mast-head…'a Rampant Cockerel, dancing round a Full Moon'… hysterically laughing saying…

"It's Lunacy!"…And,

"Oh! I can crow, wherever I go!"

"That's not even funny, Willie…"

In retaliation I worked harder, making more money to compensate for this intolerable situation until finally I snapped. We'd arranged a dinner party, with some very influential characters, a terrific bunch of raconteurs all, they could and would entertain each other for hours in a wry, self-deprecating style; that seemed entirely to elude the self-absorbed friends I later often wasted my time with!

Margot had finally met a man…she'd brought him to visit us, staying for a week. Margot introduced him as Merle…a Jazz pianist she'd met some months prior, but had surprisingly kept him under wraps. The redoubtable Willie had not hit it off with Merle, tension was in the air constantly…whiffs of 'testosterone poisoning' filled the atmosphere. Willie could often be seen standing in the doorway, with his arm up on the side of the door-jamb and one leg across the other…completely overwhelming the space, so that the 'tightly controlled' and intimidated Merle was unable to pass through! Merle had this strange habit of cracking and flexing his fingers as if he was about to play the piano…even if he was only eating a slice of toast!

Both of us had also noticed a marked change in Margot, since she'd met Merle, but it wasn't for the better…she seemed stressed and not her usual bubbly self!

There was twelve of us for dinner this night… everything was going fine 'til the 'Wild Turkey' kicked in, and Willie targeted Merle for a showdown. It was true, Merle put Margot down all the time, she couldn't do anything right! Willie wanted blood…at one point, like a 'mad-man' he'd grabbed a cigarette from the box on the table, walked across to the electric fire…ripped the fire off the wall, lit the cigarette with it, then threw it! Our guests were aghast, but nobody made a comment... Willie just sat down with the cigarette, as though this was a normal event! Then he really went to town to wind Merle into a reaction...

"What about that time in the Jacuzzi, Margot! You and me...?"

Margot was stuttering, and I could see Merle becoming puffed up and red-faced!

"We should do that again...suppose a F**k's out of the question, this time?"

Swigging back another shot of 'Wild Turkey'...I knew this was only the beginning.

"You know Merlin, sorry Merle...Margot, Arnie and me...people call us 'The Rat Pack' on account of the fact that we're so close. I'm King Rat...how d'you feel about that!"

In response Merle simply questioned the name...

"Arnie?"

"Oh! Of course, it would be typical of you to think that another man is involved....it's my pet-name for my lovely Anneka!"

In a last ditch attempt to wind Merle into a reaction, Willie leaned over to Margot in a seductive manner, making sexual gestures and growled...

"Hey! Margot, when's it gonna happen...you know what I mean?"

Margot replied...

"I don't think so baby...it would ruin the sexual tension!"

The laughter temporarily eased the situation, 'til Merle leapt across the table, smashing Margot full force in the face...her nose erupted, blood went everywhere.

In a split second, Willie grabbed Merle...dragging him across the room to the white Grand piano, near the patio window and thrust his hands under the lid, threatening to crush his fingers if he didn't beg Margot's forgiveness.

"I'll stop your handy-work, Merle...any trysts between Margot and me have always been platonic, but I love her just the same...understand this, I'll be watching you, so any sign of continued bad treatment towards Margot and I'll not stand-by and allow it to happen; certainly not from an 'over-inflated arse-hole, two-bit jazz pianist!' Do we understand each other?"

I didn't much like Merle either, but I was angry at the way Will had handled it....! Merle begged for mercy and was completely emasculated as he deserved to be. But, typically Margot stayed with him, instead of taking everyone's advice to ditch him. They married only a few months later!

I loved Willie with all my heart, but he'd become impossible...it was much later that I'd realised the reason for his unreasonable behaviour. A 'Wild Turkey' night was always going to be eventful, but the lines of 'coke' he'd secretly been using made him impossible.

After one colourful night at the Playboy Club...I'd locked him out of our flat, because of his womanizing. Whilst we'd been out...he simply drove his car right through the side of building, left the car where it stopped, and went to bed! Life between us was absolutely 'one mad episode'...completely psychedelic! Everything was 'psychedelic' dresses, shirts, ties...'life'...everything was techni-coloured. Even people's brains were psychedelic, often high on LSD!

I was tired of this round of emotion that was ripping me to bits...I wanted the world to stop and announced to Willie it was over...

"You can't mean it, Arnie?"

"I have to make a stand, Willie...*if you don't stand for something, you're bound to fall for anything*!" I screamed, in a fit of profound enlightenment!

"I hate that damn 'Void Moon'...it's cursed, I hate the way you've changed, and...er..." I stuttered...

"I hate this dreadful so called being 'in love thing' it's stinks and it hurts...and right now I hate you too!"

"Just get out of here, and get out of my life!"

Willie decided to take a long trip around the Baltic. I tried to re-organise my life with little success...I missed him beyond belief, but we had to part. At least for long enough to gather ourselves...we had torn great strips from each other's characters. In reality neither of us could deal with 'love' both harbouring a deep distrust of anything that couldn't be rationalised?

Love, this mysterious so called higher imagined emotion we'd nearly, and never quite attained, was yet another of life's imponderables!

Yet during the time we were apart I somehow came to understand 'love' or an explanation of it, that worked for me. Not the torrid tempest of 'lust' that's felt during the early throws of love, but what evolved from it! I knew we'd find a way back, I knew Willie's intellect was capable of the most superior kind of understanding. As Plato once said '*The product of intelligence, is understanding!*'

Willie and I...we could never be parted. Right now we aren't together, but we'll never be parted...

Chapter Fifteen

Willie was away for just over a year...selling 'Void Moon' after skippering her for 9 months around the Baltic, testing and expanding his nautical skills. Both of us dated other people, but with no real spark of anything remotely close to what we had together, and going about our days covering our ineffable sadness. One day whilst attempting to work, with thoughts of Willie lurking in my mind constantly, I was aware of feeling very elated, metaphorically seeing a blinding 'shaft' of illuminated realisation...as though I'd been 'shot with a diamond bullet!' This trapezoid of light lit every corner of my 'sleeping consciousness'...instantly I knew that our previous 'war of attrition' was borne out of insecurity. We simply feared each other...our attempts to destroy the other, was in fact 'in defense of being destroyed'...the logic of a lunatic, made insane by the 'power of love!'

I wanted to rush off and tell Will my new understanding! That we could work things out...until I came down to earth with a thud...he needs to understand this for himself, otherwise it's just words! We could not risk ourselves again to the evils that our jealousy of each other created. We laid to waste everything around us…but the energy of a love so fierce couldn't just die! I reassured myself.

I actually felt very calm now about everything, as though the emotion I felt for Willie had evolved to another level, a level where I wished him everything, a selfless emotion that desired nothing in return? I questioned these feelings, unable to convey them to anyone as words seemed to defy description, any meaning I felt, would be lost in the explanation?

Neither of us were tactile people, nor did the words 'I love you' quite 'cut it' as sufficiently descriptive. Proving the emotion felt between us only became possible by taking more overwhelming acts of destructive self risk, or forgiving more outrageous behavior but, in doing so would negate any respect that one was left with, for the other!

I now knew once and for all time, that I truly loved Willie Flynn…enough to be in his life any way I could, to want for him anything he wanted, or even anyone who made him happy, even another woman! This feeling was not 'settling for anything of him, at any price'…it was a meeting of minds, an understanding of the complexities that existed in a person like Will! But it would only be possible for both of us to share any relationship, as and when or if, he'd already arrived in the same place of strange mental geodesics! He was irreplaceable in my life, and life only half happened when he wasn't around!

Unbeknown to me Margot had become very close to Willie…he would go and stay with her, when Merle was away, and 'shoot the shit!' as he always called a 'Wild Turkey' night…when he'd play his most favourite music, sinking into automatic thought and babbling on about his theories of life! Or, he'd progressively turn the music up louder and louder yelling for the volume knob to be 'turned-up and torn off!' She'd patiently listened to his ramblings about the mistakes he'd made in our relationship, how he must put it right...that nobody else understood him like 'Arnie'...and on, and on 'til finally Margot said she was sick of hearing it!

Secretly deciding she'd get us together, that she'd listened enough to me and my ramblings and now Willie's to know we both felt the same way! That we were both subscribing to the same 'madness'...that our 'ravings' were beyond her understanding!

He'd become distinctively recognisable to everyone now, by the constant presence of his companion...a beautiful black, Belgium Shepherd Dog he'd called 'Jellie'...he told people 'she was the only female to love him 'warts-n-all' and never give him a bad time!' She faithfully walked by his side, everywhere he went.

Meanwhile I'd stayed a lot of the time at Gidea Park with my parents, and visiting the East End and left the cottage on Mersea Island to get quite overgrown and uncared for. I'd been tied up in work and generally keeping away from my favourite places, especially Mersea. It was time for the place to be opened and enjoyed again...Margot had agreed to come and stay, with or without Merle. I'd really missed our times together, even planning a dinner party to celebrate. The weather was beautiful on this warm summer's day...I couldn't have chosen a better time to arrange a holiday! The whole island was alive with the excitement of England defeating Germany to win the World Cup at Wembley. It was 30th July, 1966..."

"A football triumph I doubted could be repeated, at least not in my lifetime". Said old Bernie, the Shipwright!

The cottage had been cleaned, the trees, shrubs and grass cut...tables and chairs were out. Margot insisted on making her own way, having already secretly stayed the previous night at Willie's. They arrived together... there was tension for a while, but all was 'good'... Margot explained that Merle may turn up, but honestly she wasn't sure...

"Frankly my dear...I don't give a damn!"

Willie said, in a perfect 'take-off' of my favourite actor in the film 'Gone With The Wind'...Clark Gable! In a strange way, Willie was rather like the character of Rhett Butler.

Willie insisted he'd cook the evening meal saying...

"The three of us would have plenty of fun today!"...

He was an excellent cook and made cooking food not only an art but thoroughly entertaining as well! It was like old times...absolutely fabulous! A number of the 'old Mersea faces' called by and we all had drinks! The gathering grew in strength until We found ourselves 'holding court' to around 20 or so unexpected guests! The wine flowed....

Margot, in her distinct French accent and by then drunken stupor...blurted out to Willie, in front of everyone...

"William! Why you wear those ugly trousers?"

Everyone laughed, as she was talking about the fashionable 'Flared' trousers...that he was wearing, that somehow 'didn't do it' for Willie! There was always a definite sexual spark between Margot and Willie...I'd felt worried in the past, that it would become more! Was it jealousy or simply because I couldn't bear to lose either of them, or possibly both them, over an 'affair?' The three of us had spent a lot of time together as a workable threesome, we enjoyed being together, having a lot of fun together. We'd also purchased a large property in France, before our 'split-up' with a Vineyard attached to the property, which was leased to local Winemaker.

Margot mainly used the house, especially after she met Merle, but Willie and I used to go over to stay, several times a year. After Will and I sorted everything out, he never again touched 'cocaine!' Thank God!

He returned to his former fantastic self, without the aggressive outbursts...we now settled back into a real good friendship, beneath which an everlasting deep love reigned! The money was coming in and he'd wanted to get a new boat, so started to look around... he'd really wanted a Sole Bay Motor Ketch after we'd inspected a new one and read the specifications. It was a boat first designed in 1963 by J. Francis Jones and constructed in Mahogany and Larch on Oak or Canadian Rock Elm.

The Sole Bay was just right for what Willie wanted, she was bold, sheer, had an enclosed pilot-house and snug rig. She had a distinctive design, a strong 36ft Sea going yacht with a powerful diesel engine with an easy to handle, Gaff rig...

"She is a wonderful boat, she will be admired wherever she goes...a thoroughly able and handsome ship!" Willie said...

"Let's have her....Eljada!"

As soon as she was ready, we sailed Eljada from the northern Shipbuilders to Mersea Island, bringing her finally in through the 'withies' marking the channels 'til we sighted the 'Nass Beacon' before sailing into Mersea itself.

"This is fantastic, Will...I've missed sailing so much!"

"You're a 'strange fruit'...I've never known a woman, like the things you do!"

"That's me!" I replied...

"If you want 'strange fruit'...I'm your Huckleberry!" I chuckled.

"Let's all take a trip together next summer...hopefully just the three of us. If we have to suffer Merle to have Margot with us, then so be it...but if we're really lucky, he will not want to come with us...he doesn't seem to like boats, anyway!

Mersea Island is a perfect bolthole...I called it 'Mesopotamia' my secret personal name for Mersea. I came to love it more and more, so different from the jet-setting we'd done so much of in London's West End. Not only was there the partying that got too much, but the stress of constant business problems and decision making, that one needed a break from. Margot handled the French businesses which included the Paris Store, designers and the fashion shows, while I handled the UK shops.

Mersea was for Willie, the home he grew up in, but for me it was a piece of heaven, a place unlike anywhere else I'd ever been. At certain times of the day depending on the Tide Table, Mersea Island is cut off completely from the mainland for at least an hour, either side of high-tide. The island is connected to the mainland by a 'causeway' at low-tide, either side of the causeway, as far as the eye can see is an endless series of salt rivers, creeks and marshes.

Mersea Island is sandwiched between the mouth of the River Colne to the East and the River Blackwater to the West...hence my own name of 'Mesopotamia' which is Greek and translates to 'between two rivers!' At the end of the causeway when entering the island, the road forks into two very distinct and different sections of the Island. The road to the left leading to East Mersea where there are some large houses, a Country Park... even a Vineyard, and the road to the right leading to West Mersea, where we had our cottage and Will's boatshed. This winding road takes you through the village and past the very old imposing Church just before the waterfront. Course grasses cover the marsh leading down from the road to the beach itself, across little inlets through salty mud rivers, left by the receding tides.

Further along the beach are a number of house boats, with long walkways over the marsh to reach the living accommodation of the boats themselves. Then there's the boat-yard where one can hear the deafening, but wonderful orchestra of different sounds of the wood and metal of the boats' rigging, clang all day, every day.

Other sounds can be heard like that of the fishing boat engines, intermingled with the shrill of the seagulls following the boats, bringing in the fish to the sheds. Smaller boats can be seen, tending the Oyster beds, out towards the Virley Channel, past the Marina and Yacht Club. There's a camping and caravan park on the island and a couple of small tea shops; the sea front a mixture of houses and cottages, little shops and a Chandlery. It would soon be the time of year when the Regatta is staged, although it's on a different date each year, depending on the Tide, it's nevertheless, usually sometime in August. This year, we'd make sure to see the Regatta. It didn't disappoint...there was a huge Thames Barge, with distinctive dark red sails, moored in the Estuary... from which there was events like 'Walking the Plank!'

This involved bare-foot people trying to walk to the end and back, along a pole that had been greased. Most ended up in the drink, some made it to the end, but fell into the sea when attempting to walk back; it was a lot of fun. There were boat races, sponsored swims... children's sail boat races, side stalls and a fun fair. Later, a March Past of the Scottish Highlanders playing bagpipes, then to end the day...a dramatic display of fireworks, set off from the Thames Barge in the Estuary.

I was disappointed that Margot didn't arrive...I felt concerned about Margot, lately. She'd become distant, hiding herself for most of the time in France.

"Do you think something is wrong with her, Will... she doesn't answer the 'phone, and when she does, she sound very odd. Last time I spoke to her, she said that she'd grown dozens of Foxgloves...to keep all her secrets in. What does she mean, d'you think?" "Well, as if I could fathom a woman...I love Margot to bits, but I don't understand how she ticks. I must admit though, she's acting strange!"

Christmas came and we'd visited all the family had a wonderful time in the East End with Gran and Granddad, Tug, Mum and Dad...seen all our old friends. Again Margot didn't arrive...she just made excuses...she and Willie would usually chat a lot at Christmas, they had a common ground. Neither of them had family alive and adored sharing mine, chatting together about how much they missed their parents especially at Christmas. It wasn't like her to miss a Christmas stay! New Year's Day arrived...Willie and I took Eljada out to sail, regardless of the weather conditions, we always sailed on the first day, of the New Year. This would be our first New Year's trip on Eljada.

It was a bitterly cold day...as we stepped into the tender and made our way towards the boat on its mooring, in the middle of the channel. The waves were quite choppy, dashing against the side of the small tender and shooting the salty water up into the air, the severe coldness of the water making it feel like spears, as it landed on our face and heads, to feel just as though you'd been cut!

The air was sharp, invigorating and not for the feint hearted....after a while we saw several Seals swimming around the 'Nass'...

"Oh! Look Willie, over there near the Nass Beacon... Seals!"

"Arnie...do you remember that fiasco last year, after we'd taken a trip to Bradwell...one too many 'Wild Turkey' shots and I missed the 'Nass'...and ran aground. Margot slept through the whole excitement, we had to stay there, sitting lop-sided 'til the tide came in! There's something special about that Beacon...Arnie...think about it...it's been guiding people home to safety...year, upon year...since God knows when? I think I'd like my 'ashes' to go there one day!"

"Willie! Please, don't talk ridiculous!"...

Chapter Sixteen

It was 1967...we'd not seen Margot since the previous Summer, but kept trying to contact her...nobody had seen her at work, although she'd left regular instructions for the staff! Something still doesn't ring right, I've left 'phone messages...nothing at all, no response! We'd received the odd letter, saying everything in her life's 'rosie'...and for the most part, didn't question it! But, it was such a long time, without actually seeing her or speaking to her that it started to feel wrong...

"Will! I think something's very wrong...I've checked and Merle hasn't been seen either...perhaps he's gone too far in one of his rages?"

"I'm afraid Will...very afraid...I think I ought to go and find out what's happening...I don't want to call the Police, in case it's nothing. It could cause a problem with Merle, if he thinks I'm spying!"

Willie adored Margot and insisted on coming with me, there was also the deep fear and possibility in Will's mind that Merle might, cut up rough with me, as well as Margot. If he's with me then he can deal with Merle. I was very glad he'd be coming for that reason alone; plus I'd sensed trouble...a feeling of doom haunted me...I needed his support! We prepared to leave for France, stocked the boat, packed some clothes and arranged for Will's dog Jellie to stay with Mum and Dad at Gidea Park.

Just before we left there was a desperate telephone call from Margot...another minute's difference and I wouldn't have been at the cottage. Picking up the receiver to hear Margot sobbing down the 'phone...

"Help me, help me...I've killed Merle...he's dead, Annie...I've stabbed him!"

"Oh! God, Margot!"

...screaming out to Willie, to come quick! It's Margot, she says, Merle's dead...she's stabbed him! Grabbing the 'phone he asked her whether she'd called an ambulance or the police...she had! It was only a matter of time before she would be arrested. Willie told her to wait 'til we'd arranged for a lawyer to represent her, before saying anything. We would get there as soon as we could.

"Annie, I don't know why I'm saying this, but I want 'you' to fly across to Margot. I'm going to sail over in Eljada, theres things I want to arrange in the East End first. I want to arrange a Passport for Margot in case we can get her out of France! Try everything you can to get her out on Bail...and make sure to get the best Lawyer money can buy. I always knew that Merle was a 'dangerous character'...he just 'oozed bad vibes!' God knows what Margot suffered to resort to this....why didn't she tell us?"

I felt worried about his idea, but brushed it aside.

Upon reaching Paris, I went straight to the Lawyer's office to be greeted by a short, thin Frenchman named Jules Dubuisson who explained the situation.

"Your friend Margot Le Queux has been charged with the murder her husband Merle Le Queux...but, there are grounds to argue Crime Passionel!"

"Crime Passionel....what does that mean? Is it 'crime of passion!" I queried. "Yes....the facts suggest, she was pushed to her limits of mental endurance by her husband...there wasn't any pre-meditation in her actions. His violence also caused her to mis-carry their child...his continued abuse, she just snapped! I cannot tell you any more of the case at this time, but I am doing my best to get her out...are prepared to stand 'bond' and be responsible for her? I will keep everything as simple as I can....rather than confuse you with French legalities!"

"Yes! Yes, of course!" I replied in stunned amazement...

She was pregnant? My thoughts were everywhere... 'she hadn't even told us!'

"When can I see her?" I pleaded.

"That's not possible for the moment...but, if everything goes well, in the next couple of days we will know whether the case can proceed, without her being imprisoned during the Trial!"

Leaving Jules Dubuisson's office at around 5pm with the Paris traffic heavier than usual, I travelled the seemingly endless journey to the chateau with my head painful with thoughts of Margot. My wonderful friend... all I could see was her little...elfin body, her big generous smile and warm heart; her infectious giggles and her powerful, dynamo of a character. In fact I often commented to people who hadn't met her that she was very similar to Edith Piaf...tiny, powerful...a very beautiful person.

"What will become of her, what will happen now...I hope Willie doesn't take too long to get here!" I said aloud.

I felt the tears welling up as I thought of little Margot, all alone...trying to deal with that brute, Merle. He was built like a 'brick-shit house'...he was a bully!

"Oh! Why didn't she tell us...why didn't we pay more attention...why, why?"

I was so wound up that I screamed these words at the top of my voice...as I was going into the chateau. I would stay in the annexe to the chateau which was used as the servants' quarters...I'll try and find out from them, what's been going on.

I had little joy, finding out anything that I didn't already know...he bullied Margot. Then cut her off from friends, sacked the staff...keeping her a prisoner from everything and everyone. None of the previous employees, knew anything about Margot being pregnant? A girl named Marie had previously worked for Margot the longest...she said she'd been worried, but could do nothing...! She at least was more than happy to come back and work, whilst the case proceeded. I was very grateful for a friendly face, she would come at 8am the next day...I would unpack, shower, eat and have an early night and think clearly in the morning. I still wasn't sure how long it would take Will to see certain people in the East End! It would have to be all arranged via 'Tug' anyway. What would be his response? I hope he'll put Willie right...I don't think it's a good idea to try and get her out of France...but I'm so confused about everything! It's all just a nightmare...perhaps I'll wake up soon!

The morning broke, bright and sunny with not a cloud in the sky....it was 12th July, 1967, so much for the 'swinging sixties!' I scoffed. Putting on a pot to boil, I made some fresh coffee and walked out into the garden, sitting at the patio table. The garden was glorious, a blaze of colour...absolutely dozens and dozens of Foxgloves, they were simply beautiful. I looked over to the right near the main house where I could just see an area sectioned off by police notices. Forensics' officers were still working in and around the area, with a sort of tent erected? I looked away not wanting to think about what they were digging for.

It was only a few days since receiving the news of this whole tragic business, but it already seemed a lifetime. I expect it will be a good week or so before Willie actually gets here...I wished he'd flown with me...I can't stand this constant muttering to myself...I feel slightly mad, in fact, more than slightly! The weekend approaching I couldn't even get news from Jules Dubuisson...still, we'll know the score on Monday. I slept fitfully over those days...perhaps Margot would be able to make a 'phone call, but I heard nothing.

Monday morning, found me pacing about outside Dubuisson's office door...it wasn't far from the Court building so I figured he would go there first. He arrived and bumbled about in a manner that my imagination pictured, as a sort of Dicken's character.

"Hmm! It's a good thing he comes highly recommended!" I thought...

"He really doesn't do much to inspire my confidence; but then what do I know?"

He explained that there was no medical records to confirm Margot's pregnancy...that apparently, when she mis-carried, Merle wouldn't call for an ambulance, nor allow her to have ante-natal care when she first knew of the pregnancy. The 6 month foetus is buried in the garden. Margot named the baby girl Chantelle, after her Mother. She has a photograph that she secretly took of the baby, and hid from Merle. She keeps repeating *"Ecce Crucem Domini"*...

"Yes, I've heard her say that before...it means 'Behold the Cross of the Lord'...she would quote it, when she needed strength!" I confirmed.

It was now a week since it happened...Willie would arrive any time!

The Court Proceedings went very slowly, especially as I didn't really understand much of what was said. It was truly a time I regretted knowing so little French. Journalists were waiting about like 'Vultures' for the story and the pictures...my eyes constantly darting back and forth across the large room, watching first one lawyer speak, then Jules Dubuisson, watching their 'body language' for clues.

Suddenly, one of the large double doors opened and Willie blustered in, breathing a huge sigh of relief that he'd found the right place...there was a moment of silence as the people fixed a disapproving gaze at him. 'Thank God!' I thought, gesturing to him to sit down anywhere, as soon as possible...these French Lawyers, spare no time for trifling interruptions. Neither of us knew, what the hell was going on...every so often Willie and I would look at each other as our names were mentioned; eyes wide and vacant of understanding. Was all going well, or not?

The Judge stood up abruptly, everyone else did the same...it seemed to be over? Margot was taken down some stairs and through a little opening, her eyes looking back at us, pleadingly! I feared the worst...Jules approached, so did Willie. The court has allowed her out, but into our care. She has to give up her Passport and we're to stand bond 'til the Trial!

Chapter Seventeen

A rriving at the chataeu…Willie put his limited clothes he'd brought away, and proceeded to go through the servant's quarters with a 'fine toothed comb' destroying anything remotely described as medication. Margot had some sleeping pills, which Willie would look after and give her, himself. Knives were locked away, and we made sure she was never left alone. We ate an adequate meal, making sufficient conversation to try and keep an equilibrium…'til finally Margot went to bed. She slept simply because of the sleeping pills.

Sure that Margot was sound asleep we gave vent to everything we felt about the whole drama.

"To think, Willie…we've modelled and had our photographs on Insurance Policy brochures, for the 2.4 semi-detached suburban Mr. Jones's; posed and been photographed to illustrate the perfect 'package holiday' in glossy brochures…and now involved in a murder nightmare…I can't believe, it's all happened?"

"Yeah!…I should've punched that bastard, Merle, when I had the chance…I always knew he was a low-life…'lower than a snake, in a wagon rut!' Should've made sure he went straight out of Margot's life!"

"She never spoke a word of what's happened...did she? She seems to be in a trance...going through the motions, like a robot. It's just the beginning, how's she gonna cope?"

"We could take her out of here...away from France... I've got the Passport done!

"We could leave anytime, now even, drive to where the boat is moored, set sail before she awoke!" Willie said, with blinding prescience...in total committed belief that it was the answer.

"No!...Absolutely, No! It's a not an option!"

I demanded, with an air of some control.

"Will, I know you love Margot and want to save her, but she would not want this dealt with this way...we must give her some time to talk about all this...and... well...Jules Dubuisson feels she has a very good chance, with her Defence of 'Crime of Passion!' " "Maybe, you're right!"

Willie's faced looking downhearted.

"I've arranged for Marie to come, you remember Marie, worked for Margot for years. Anyway, I've arranged for her to be here early in the morning...around 7am. We can have breakfast then arrange to see Jules at his office. He can fill you in on the 'legal situation' discuss everything properly...we can get all the business messages sorted, then concentrate on Margot!"

"Okay...you've got it all worked out, sounds sensible, but you know how I hate, sensible!"

Will's agreed, reluctantly that it was the right course to take. Talking with Margot, the next morning, she seemed quite cheerful given the circumstances...she hugged Willie, then me...repeatedly.

"I love you, both...so much!"

She said...waving to us as we finally left...with tears in her eyes.

"She will be alright with Marie...I've told her, not to go out and leave her!"

I said to Will...as much to reassure myself as anything.

"I can't help feeling afraid...she seems, somehow strange...still, once we've sorted everything out, we can be with her all the time!"

Relieved to be back, having done the jobs planned, we turned into the drive...all was quiet. Proceeding through into the garden, we found Marie sitting at the patio table. Margot was lying out on the lawn, down near the flower beds, sunbathing.

"How's she been, Marie?"

"Fine...she, put on a swimsuit, a sunhat and sunglasses, took some juice and her writing box. She was writing a letter for a while then she did a bit of gardening...then she laid down to sunbath. I've not taken my eyes off her...all the time you were out, as you asked!"

Willie and I sat down at the table and poured a cold drink...Marie went off to make lunch. We left Margot to rest a while longer...

"You know if all this hadn't happened, we'd be on our sailing trip. Margot said last year when we planned it, she would come...whether Merle wanted to or not! But...I think she just said that to cover the fact that she couldn't make a move without his say so...he controlled her. That's obvious!"

Marie came out with a tray of salad, an assortment of cheeses, French bread and a bottle of Cotes du Rhone. I called out to Margot...there was no response.

"Margot...Marie's made some lunch!"

Still no response...a cold sense of alarm washed over me, and I rushed towards her. Willie and Marie... followed in quick succession. Her hat was over her face, as though to shield it from the sun...I moved it with my heart racing. I screamed out in horror as I saw the leaves and Foxglove flower blooms, stuffed in her mouth. Evidence of vomit each side of her head...with leaves and pieces of the blooms in it...one hand still clutching crushed flowers, and the other holding a letter.

I grabbed her face, pulling the leaves and flowers out of her mouth, calling to her to wake up.

"Oh! Margot...please wake up...someone call an ambulance. Willie help me get her up on her feet...we'll make her walk. Margot, Margot...no, don't leave us!"

Sobbing and screaming hysterically...my tears dropping on to her lifeless body.

"She's gone darling, Annie...she's gone!"

Willie said, clutching her wrist...there's no pulse... tears now gushing silently down his face.

"No! No! She can't be!"

The ambulance came, they took her, but she was already dead...the letter she'd been clutching, was now lying on the blanket. It was addressed to me and Willie. I picked it up and held it close to my chest, unopened... as though to be close to her...not really wanting to know the contents yet at the same time compelled. The shock was too much at the moment to cope with knowing her last thoughts. I just held the letter close, in disbelief.

In the course of just over a week...the whole world had changed, forever. Marie was sobbing too...Willie poured us all a drink, while we waited for the police. Nobody spoke or uttered a single sound.

The Police came...there would be an enquiry, but it's clear that it was suicide by poisoning using '*Digitalis purpurea*' or Foxgloves...self-ingested. Apparently these plants are highly toxic with every part of the plant being poisonous, reacting in only 20 to 30 minutes. My mouth dropped open as the Policeman was explaining.

"It all makes sense now...she's been talking about these flowers for some time. Willie, do you remember me saying...how she said, the blooms held all her secrets?"

We finally decided to read the letter, but first poured ourselves a drink. I insisted that Willie read it aloud.

'To my Dearest Friends...Anneka and Willie,

I hope you will find it in your hearts to forgive me for what I've done.

For me it was the only way. You must not blame yourselves. I had already decided to do this a long time ago, when I first read about Foxgloves being highly toxic.

There were times when I planned to poison Merle, but I coul'nt carry it out, especially when I found out I was pregnant. Merle once again, let me down... killing our baby, with his violence. I stabbed him in grief, not even realising that he would die.

He'd killed our little Chantelle, and I couldn't forgive it.

My life has been destroyed and if it wasn't for you 'guys'...it would have seemed pointless too.

I love you both...thank you for being always in my life, and never letting me down.

We always had such great times, I want to always be with you.

Do you remember the great times sailing, when we'd run aground after having too much fun with a drink or several of either Champagne or in Willie's case...'Wild Turkey' and missing the 'Nass Beacon' at Mersea.

Our Annie started calling it the 'Nasty Beacon'...instead of the Nass.

Do you remember Willie, that you said you wanted your Ashes to go there one day...

Annie was furious...saying you're too young to talk like that, don't be ridiculous.

Well I decided then, secretly...that's where I would have my Ashes put, around the 'Nass Beacon' to be near my friends...forever in 'Mesopotamia'

I have left everything I own to you both to share, as you know I have no family.

You both have always been my family. Please do everything you can to arrange for Chantelle's Ashes to be with me.

I'll rely on you to make this happen...I know you will, because you're both determined people and because you know it means everything to me. Please don't feel sad for me, or grieve too much...try please to remember me with a smile, as I am thinking of you both and smiling now...as I write this letter.

I have kissed this letter twice.

A kiss for both of you, I am so glad I hugged you both this morning...to my sleep now I go, without fear in the knowledge that I'm loved by you both. Loved by the best...so my thanks...

All my love from us, in this world and the next,
Margot and Chantelle xx

Willie choked back the tears and had to stop reading it several times...I was sobbing at all the beautiful words she'd written.

"I wish so much I could hug her now, Willie...nothing will seem the same. We must make sure we honour her wishes, not matter what it takes, or how long it takes. God knows what red tape it'll involve. I'll speak to Jules Dubuisson...they'll be a lot to do. I can't think about it now. Tomorrow! We'll have to deal with everything, tomorrow!"

Chapter Eighteen

It was a small Ceremony...all the staff came, and we decided the Paris store would be closed that day. A number of friends travelled over from Mersea Island, Colchester and the West End. My brother Bill came, with Mum and Dad...Gran' and Granddad, travelled from the East End with 'Tug'...she would have been so pleased. Everyone that knew Margot simply fell in love with her. I was comforted by the fact that she'd be travelling back with us, on Eljada...we would still take her on the trip we'd planned, the previous year. We'd probably be setting out around the end of August.

Just as the service was ending, I'd noticed...Willie look across...he smiled and nodded. He loved me...I knew it!

I smiled back...he knew, he was loved, too! That was the way we were...

We set sail from Calais to cross the channel to Dover...it was a clear day, and the sea state was calm. We would probably find a berth in the Marina for a night or two in Dover, before moving on around the coast towards home.

As we lost sight of Calais and all we could see was the ocean, I felt that old sense of exhilaration return. There was nothing else in the world that had that effect on me...so exciting, the sounds of the rigging, the wind in the sails and every so often the seagulls. The waves dashing at the sides of the boat as she cut through the water. We often didn't speak for hours, we knew each other and what was required when sailing...we'd just get on with it. Other times I'd sit myself in the small seat in the corner of the wheelhouse...Willie would set the auto-navigator on course and then we'd chat. Every so often you'd hear the navigator make a winding sound, as it pulled us back on the set course. Even when the weather was hot, it could feel quite cold out in the middle of the channel, it was great to be able to sit snug in the wheelhouse, with the sliding doors shut. Nothing else in the world mattered at that time, it was us two and a boat, crossing the sea with the raw nature of the beast, ready to test you with its power...any time it felt like it! The Sea commanded total respect, unless you're a fool...

We eventually sighted the white cliffs...then, the dark rock of the walls, built during the Napoleonic wars to enclose and protect the entrance to Dover Harbour. Willie called over the radio 'ship to shore'...

"Eljada to coastguard...! Over...!"

The coastguard responded, with instructions and permission to enter the Harbour. Once in we hired a berth and moored...brewed some tea, we then went for a walk. Land were reality reigned...I didn't need too much more reality at the moment! We walked silently and pensive still trying to rationalise the traumatic recent events and what we would do next. Would we sail on further, round into the Solent...or head straight back towards home? We ate and settled for the night.

The morning broke, it was really warm, the sun bright and I felt more cheerful…saying good morning to Margot and Chantelle, who's ashes sat safely clamped on the chart table in an earthenware pot!

"I'd really like to take a walk around the Castle, Will!"

"Okay, let's do it…"

We set out up the winding roads to find different pathways leading up the cliffs, higher and higher. The views out over the Harbour from the cliffs, spectacular…the Ferries looked so small from here…when in fact, they are quite colossal. We spent all day exploring this historic and fantastic Castle…

"It's amazing isn't it Will…we are treading ground that's been trod by men of war…ghosts of which are all around us…it gives me a strange feeling!"

"That's because you're strange, Arnie!"

"C'mon…I'll race you up that hill!"

Willie grabbed my hand and pulled me up….we started to run…'til we were both puffing and blowing for England…totally 'out of breath!' Then we slumped ourselves down on the grass to rest.

We talked and talked…in the guileless spillage of old secrets. Like two old enemy sailors, that had just learnt they were born from the same woman…brothers by blood. Nothing in the world could ever change the ineluctable bond, mysteriously formed during this voyage. We had profound conversations and silly conversations…we laughed and cried about good times, and toasted absent friends. If we lived a millions years we could learn no more, than we'd just learnt of each other's depths, strengths and weaknesses…giving due respect to all these qualities…and a silent promise, never to abuse them.

We walked through the castle with the ghosts of the past, down the cliff path with the breeze of the present, to sail tomorrow with the winds...into the future. Somehow, the events of the last weeks had made everything in our thoughts, sharp and crystal clear, life more tangible...the grass seemed greener, the sky more blue. The world full of inestimable riches of nature... previously missed by the stresses of life, and the futility of making money that couldn't be enjoyed, beyond what was needed to live.

The evening sky became the most magnificent orange, we sat on the deck of Eljada with a plate of grilled Sardines, French bread and a bottle of Chablis...charging our glasses; we drank to 'life!'

"I think we should sail on to Queensborough tomorrow...what d'you think, Arnie?" "Yep...! Sounds good to me, Skipper...!"

We had a fry-up to start the day, then sailed out through the Strait of Dover to follow the coastline about a mile or so offshore. We sailed onwards through the Goodwin Sands and, round the North Foreland to Margate. Along and across The Swale...hopefully, we would be into Queensborough around midday, if we're lucky...depending on whether the Sea is with us or not. Whether we use the engine or went with the sails...we would go with the flow and decide as we travelled. This trip would have no pressures...there was no rush. I found myself telling Margot about the journey, talking to her as if she was there in person...and wondered about her presence. I was sure I'd smelt her perfume at times, and felt her hand brush against my face?

It couldn't be my imagination...it would be hard to imagine any other smells on a boat! As any sailor would know...the smells onboard, are boat smells...engine oil, rope, wood, sea water and more than a hint of dampness. I brewed some tea and sat drinking it in the wheelhouse, as we rounded Sheerness, into the Medway to Queensborough and moored...it was very peaceful, and I was thoughtful.

There was a silence everywhere just a gentle lapping sound of the water hitting the boat...the sun shining down on the deck. We laid ourselves down to doze... lulled by the gentle swaying motion, in the warmth of the afternoon sun. I was aware that I didn't want the journey to end, even though we were taking Margot and Chantelle home to their final resting place. The journey seemed somehow spiritual, celestial and almost not of this world...I looked at Will, long and hard in absolute terror of the day he may not be there! We've come full circle over the years, through our passions, love and sometimes hate...to arrive in a place too special to lose...he's unique as a man, irreplaceable as my friend and partner! He must have felt my eyes boring into him...he turned and looked at me, puzzled for a moment, then smiled!

I felt a sudden shudder...I didn't dare question what it meant, but I was sure it was an 'omen!'

At times I was convinced Willie was a Warlock...he roared with laughter when I told him so...he always seemed to know, what I was thinking...this time was no exception; he leapt up from the deck and across to me in one swift movement, ruffling my hair about and telling me not to worry, he wasn't going anywhere! I laughed nervously...as he said in one of his affectionate little jibes!

"Come here...Silly old bag...!" Hugging me tight...!

"I've told you, I'm not going anywhere...so take that worried look off your face and give me a smile. Okay!"

Willie busied about the boat, tidying ropes...shaking and folding the sails to tie down and clearing the decks. I cleaned up inside the boat, before preparing something to eat...Willie suddenly leapt down the steps, into the galley.

"Out of the way...I'm 'galley slave' today. I'm going to rustle-up a feast...you can sit and keep me company. Yeah! And open that bottle of Rioja!"

I wasn't about to argue...he was much better at cooking than me, and the entertainment value was 'second to none!' He'd always have a white tea towel over his arm while he spun the pots, tapped the utensils in melodic beats...throwing the food in the air, to catch in whatever cooking pan he was using. His body language when cooking was an art-form, almost a choreographed dance, it was the same when he was doing a gig as a Disc Jockey, it was true enjoyment and a performance of unadulterated self-indulgent fun that infected everyone else! Every so often he'd thrust a piece of food into my mouth...

"Good...?"

"Very good...!"

He'd cooked a particular favourite of mine. One of his specialty dishes ...'Beef Stroganoff'.

"Thank you darling. You're my hero!"

We ate on deck and afterwards sat with our legs dangling over the side of the boat, reminiscing...

"Hey! Will...do you remember the time...you, me and Margot were on 'Void Moon' with some friends in St. Tropez...and you said to everyone, completely on impulse 'Who wants to see the Galapagos Islands?' They all cheered and foolishly said 'Yeah, let's go!' Next thing, we set sail....two days of sailing and partying later, they realised you meant it! But, you wouldn't let them off...we made way for the Galapagos, off Ecuador... then, you changed your mind and headed instead through the Panama Canal into the Caribbean. Finally, we drifted into harbour in Kingston, Jamaica...having frightened everyone to death by sailing on through a storm! The three of us laughed and laughed...especially when they all got off, refusing to get back onboard with a bunch of lunatics!"

"Yeah...Arnie, and what about that 'cool dude' French guy, Pierre...he'd been after Margot for months before that trip. He'd constantly pursued her, wooing her at every possible opportunity...but, he couldn't get off that boat fast enough, as well! Remember, Margot calling out to him...laughing and mocking at the same time...

"Pierre...leaving me so soon...you said it was true love!"

Good times...Port Antonio was fantastic...could've stayed there longer. Never did see that bunch again...I reckon they kept a watch for us, making their escape whenever they saw us sail into St. Tropez!"

We laughed about these stories 'til our faces hurt and the darkness descended, the moon was full, casting a huge reflection in the quivering gentle waves. Willie suddenly said with a sigh...

"That boat was great, but you were right, it was too big, and the name was tempting providence...'Void Moon'...many times there were strange goings on...I'd wondered a few times, whether she was haunted?"

I broke in..."What shall we do tomorrow, stay another night here, or move on?

Shouldn't have asked really...

"You're going to do that 'Gone With The Wind'... 'Tara, Tara...tomorrow's another day'...thing! Okay, we'll decide in the morning."

The decision was made for us the next morning... thick dark clouds, hung ominously in the sky. Silently eating breakfast...at different times, both of us looked across to the 'earthenware pot' containing Margot and Chantelle's Ashes, with an ache at the miss of her. We set sail, leaving the mouth of the Medway to sail across the mouth of the Thames to the Shoeburyness coastline. The sea was coming up choppy and it was now raining hard as we sailed towards Maplin Sands. I checked to make sure the hatchways had been battened down.

By the time we reached Foulness Point near the mouth of the River Crouch Eljada was being tossed high in the air and crashing down in the void, as the swell of the waves disappeared from under the hull of the boat. The storm had blown up fast...the thunder smashed, sounding like the skies were splitting open, lightning zig-zagged across it...the waves came up in huge three metre swells, that seemed to just be about to tip the boat over...when Eljada would smash down and right itself.

"Shall we try and get in to Burnham...or sail on through?" Willie shouted.

"Let's not get sensible now, Willie....keep going, sail on through. Once we get through Buxey Sands, we're almost home, and the Tide's with us...just keep going Will's...keep going!"

Willie battled with Eljada through the storm, which gradually began to subside as we approached the

Blackwater. With the suddenness that the storm had started, it stopped. The sun came out and the sea calmed and there in view was the Nass Beacon. We looked at each other...

"I'd like to take Margot's Urn home with us first... we've always been 'people of the night'...it'd like to 'cast the ashes' in the moonlight!"

We both agreed.

It was a beautiful warm, cloudless, Moonlit night... climbing into the tender, with the evanescent green shimmering algae, luminously glowing...lit by the slightest of movements in the water. We climbed from the tender and onto Eljada then cast off to head towards our 'Nass Beacon' it was too emotional...there were no words!

We silently released the 'Ashes' into the waves....

Chapter Nineteen

Christmas 1967 was a big affair, the loss of Margot brought home to me the importance of the people I cared about...I wanted to see everyone, and party for England with friends and family. We really had endless fun and saw to it that everyone else had fun too. Christmas Eve, we'd booked for a large party, around 100 friends and family to dine. It was a ritual to dine out at the George Hotel in Colchester's High Street on Christmas Eve which we did each year, but this year was the biggest. It was a great night, some people made it home, others stayed in the Hotel. Some had other plans for Christmas Day, but most were coming home to Mersea Island for a few days, then we were heading to the East End for the New Year celebrations.

"We must make sure to get back in time to sail Eljada on New Year's Day...especially as I have Margot's parcel!"

"What are you talking about, woman?" Willie said, with a wry smile on his face.

"It's a collection of little Christmas bits, from the crackers, a card from us to Margot and Chantelle, also some Christmas Pudding...I've burned them in the grate, and put the ashes in this little box. We can take them to the Nass on New Year's Day."

It promised to be a good year, and 1968 started with many plans, money was still plentiful, although we would sell off all the French business connections. Fashion, music and life in general promised to be very exciting, and the sixties are still swinging. There was even talk of putting a 'man on the moon' before the end of the decade. It would certainly be a decade I'd never forget.

We planned to sail off to the Mediterranean and generally see as much of the world as possible. Willie spent a lot of time working in his boatshed and working on Eljada. The dog, Jellie would be with him all the time, even if he was on the boat moored in the Estuary, Jellie would sit on the beach looking out to the boat, until he returned. She was such a faithful dog and was totally her master's baby.

Willie only had to give a whistle and she was there immediately, wagging her tail. Mum and Dad came to stay for a week in February, the week of my 27th Birthday. Dad and Willie took Eljada out most days, and in the evening would spread the sea charts over the floor; they'd chat about all sorts of boy's stuff, history, boats, psychology...everything, but the war. Dad only ever spoke about to war, exclusively to Uncle George, otherwise the subject was taboo.

On the last day of their visit we sailed across to Bradwell-on-Sea and into the Marina, had a few leisurely drinks in the Yacht Club then looked around the Bradwell Lodge where there's a Bird Observatory.

After that went on to take a look at St. Peter's Saxon Chapel (AD 654), then to a small pub for a meal. It was very cold, the wind biting, everywhere looked forlorn as we made our way back to the marina and set sail back across the Virley Channel, several times I noticed beads of sweat appearing on Will's brow, and puzzled about it. We waved Mum and Dad off the next day and Willie went to meet some friends while I caught up with some paper-work.

I felt ill at ease lately, I had no explanation for it; I would turn expecting to see someone but there'd be nobody! I would feel someone touch me or smell perfume. I'd hear a bird fluttering behind the mirror, hanging over the fireplace and check the chimney when the fire wasn't alight. But still hear the bird, whether the fire alight or not? I was sure that it was the Banshees...but what could I do? I brushed off these feelings believing it was my imagination, although constantly haunted.

It was March now and it snowed, a layer of a few inches settled across the front garden, the road and pavement was white, and out across the marshes. The virgin snow glistened as the sun came out to gradually melt it away...it was the 15th March and we were expecting company for dinner. We loved dinner parties and they were always unpredictable; sometimes the evening would be spent chatting or debating current issues round the table, or turn into a raucous party without warning or planning...just evolved with the mood. One of Willie's former girlfriends came; Tessa, like most of his old girlfriends kept in touch as we were all civilised friends. In truth, all of us probably slightly nuts...none of our friends were what 'one' might call ordinary! It was the best night for a long time, we ate, talked...even sang and danced. It was really rare to get Willie to dance, but we danced that night, I hadn't even prompted him. He told everyone about our planned sailing trip to the Mediterranean...

"I can't remember when I've been more excited about a trip before!"

He said, pouring himself a 'Wild Turkey'...his chosen tipple.

Heaven knows what time everyone left, but it wasn't important as everyone lived on the Island and just stumbled home. Tessa would probably be in one of the spare rooms or staying over with Andrew, on the houseboat across the road to the beach. By the time I awoke, the house was quiet and completely empty... everywhere was cleaned and tidy. I don't know how he's does it I thought...I only have to have a few glasses of red wine and I'm thoroughly ill. Willie can 'tie one on'...have a 'Wild Turkey' night and still get up early...I bet he's down that boatshed already. I'll take him some lunch later. The 'phone rang a number of times it was friends thanking us for a brilliant night. I leisurely took a shower and got ready and made some lunch. I smelt that perfume again, and mumbled to myself...

"If I didn't know better...I'd think Margot was here!"

Packing the lunch and including hot soup, I put on my thick coat, scarf and hat and set off to walk the half-mile to the boatshed...'it seems very quiet!' I thought. Willie's usually banging about, making plenty of noise...he just 'doesn't do quiet!' I felt a sudden wave of trepidation and hesitated before opening the door, drawing breath to find Willie slumped over his desk, with Jellie sitting by his side.

"No! Willie...No! Please God! Let him be okay?"

Screaming....as I picked up the 'phone and dialed for an ambulance. I grabbed his face, he was cold...

"Oh! No! He can't be...!"

I fell to the ground, sobbing...'til someone came.

The Cremation Service was a sort of dream to me, as though in a daze...how it all got organised or how everyone knew is a mystery, but around 200 people attended. Many of them old girlfriends, all with a story to tell of 'naughty' things he'd done when they'd dated him! It may sound crazy, but I kept thinking...'He'd be enjoying every minute of this! He'd be laughing at all these stories!' His send off in 'death' was as unique, as the 'man' was in life...it all couldn't have been more appropriate, if he'd staged it himself!

There was nothing insignificant about Willie...he was loved by most, controversial, complex, fiery and certainly never 'invisible' to anyone! He never simply came into a room, he arrived to make an entrance with gusto...the force of his personality was such, that it was as if a switch had turned on a hundred light bulbs at once...everyone knew when Willie was about! If you couldn't see him, you'd hear his distinctive strong voice or laugh, that boomed above everyone else's.

His life was a master-class. He saw the world through 'binoculars'...when the rest of the world wore 'bifocals!' His devastating wit and attitudes, were often 'Machiavellian!' And, if anyone ever called him 'nice' he'd laugh and say...

"Nice! Nice! Who wants to be nice? Nice is Magnolia! Why be 'nice' when you can be 'naughty?'"

Yes! He was 'naughty' a very naughty boy...but the best! A techni-coloured character, great company, utterly irreverent, full of life and fun!

There are these last things to say. At dinner on that last night before Willie died, he'd said the strangest thing, for reasons I cannot now recall. He'd said...

"I hope it is said of me, when I'm gone...that I was always true to myself!"

Yes! I can confirm this of him...'Willie was always true to himself!'

His Ashes went to the 'Nass Beacon'...Mesopotamia!

After Will's ashes were scattered from Eljada I left the boat on her mooring. Since then, more than one person has said they've seen him standing in the wheelhouse!

The rest of 1968 was bad, the grief was terrible...I thought it couldn't get any worse. But it did...on the 19th December, 1968 my brother Bill and I lost our beloved Dad, and Mum lost her loving husband. The Cremation Service took place on Christmas Eve...

> Our Dad, was one of the Nation's Heroes...
> He was our Hero...
> No! He was more...he was 'our Dad!'

My thoughts are that 'one' cannot measure the emotional cost or the grief of loving people so deeply, that the pain is so intolerable! That each day is a living death, and each thought is like a spear piercing the mind, the heart and the very soul, every part of the body hurts! Even though you know they're gone from the physical world... you see their face in every window, in every car, in every crowd...across every room, and feel their presence everywhere, and in everything you do.

It was a very long time before this pain, turned to thoughts of happy times and joy, but it did...eventually!

Christmas was not much of a celebration, nor was the New Year of 1969. I sold all my business interests and decided to completely change my life, to start again in the new decade of 1970 in a different way. The 1970's onwards would be different, but always with the best of memories of Dad and a wonderful family.

I felt suddenly...startled and disorientated. As though I'd dreamed a long dream...remembering the amazing times shared with Margot and Flynn, Willie Flynn... who'll walk with me, forever.

I will be remembering always...'the Ashes of Nass Beacon'.

The End

A Personal Note
from the Author

I wrote the first draft of 'Murder...The Ashes of Nass Beacon' in 2005. In fact, I finished it on Westley's birthday, the 18th August, 2005. However, on the 12th September, 2005 due to having received the shock news that Westley had been fatally stabbed, was unable to bring myself to revisit the book draft until now. The time felt right this year to work on the book again, dedicate it to Westley and raise much needed funds for the Charity, founded in his memory. I would like to take the opportunity of thanking my family for their support and courage in dealing with the challenges faced. Also, to share some thoughts about the affects this tragedy has had on our family and the subsequent work since.

Being born into a large extended family I became aware of the death of people I loved from a very early age and, the sadness it brings in knowing I would never see them again. No doubt for many of you reading these words...the 'passing' or death of a 'loved-one' is something taken for granted as an event that happens during the normal journey of life, through old age or illness!

We are used to seeing horrors daily on the TV news... life taken prematurely, through tragic accidents, war, terrorism or even through murder! I'm sure most people can recall where they were and what they were doing when 9/11 happened. I particularly remember the 9/11 newsflash and Westley calling out to me...

"Oh! My God! Mum, come and see this...! Quick, quick...!"

This shocking event will remain vivid in me, marking time, not only because of the magnitude of what I was witnessing but, the memory of Westley being here at home with me, when this happened!

We tend to view these horrors with sympathy for the bereaved families but, mostly with little real understanding of what 'traumatic death' really means to those left behind, grieving?

Often, the event passing quickly from thought! Sadly, happening to other people!

Something 'we' have no power to do anything about!

During the summer of 2005, just as I was about to finish the first draft of writing this book, my Mother and I took a trip down memory lane, visiting seaside places she had been to as a child, places I remembered as a child too. Finally, deciding to stay in a small Hotel we'd found in Margate. It was a particularly good summer that year, little rain and lots of sunshine! Our plan was to have a break for a week, then be back home to celebrate Westley's 27th Birthday, on the 18th August. Westley, was born the middle child of my three, now adult children.

After settling ourselves in to the small coastal Hotel...I set off to get few provisions from the nearby shop. Puzzled to see lots of flowers on the ground outside the shop...it was soon evident that they were 'not for sale?' I felt an immediate lurch of my stomach, instinctively experiencing a sense of sadness. Curiosity finally got the better of me and as I reached the young girl at the till I said…

"I hope you'll forgive me for intruding, but may I ask why there are flowers on the ground outside the shop?"

Before the young girl could answer, a small lady came alongside me, her tears clearly visible…

"Thank you for asking. They are for my Son…he came home after a night out with his friends. The next day we found him dead in bed. Police think it was because of a drugs overdose! We are still waiting to hear!"

My heart sank and I remember taking her hand with the words choking in my throat…

"I'm so, so sorry for the loss of your precious Son! As a mother myself I can't begin to imagine the pain you must be feeling at losing a child! I'm so very sorry!" Little could I have known that I too would soon have first-hand understanding of her suffering and grief, only weeks later? I have thought of her often since.

I remember the sun was shining bright on the morning of the 12th September, 2005, it was a Monday, a day my whole family will never forget! It was warm and bright all day…but, by 3pm in the afternoon 'Westley's life had been stolen!' He'd been fatally stabbed in an unprovoked attack at a cash machine.

The evil hand of homicide 'a mindless act of violence'… our lives would never be the same again…bringing with it a veil of darkness. So powerful is the grief…that literally, the world seemed 'black and white' totally devoid of colour. It is traumatic, all-consuming, a grief like no other. Grief, that results in overwhelming pain which is everything on the spectrum. Indescribable pain that is emotional, physical, as well as psychological. The subsequent feelings of isolation making 'one' feel insignificant...a 'shadow' of one's former self! The whole family seemed to 'flounder' in a state of bewilderment!

We found ourselves 'fast-tracked' into another world...a world of questions! Some questions that could be answered and far too many that couldn't because of Subjudice! Worse still are the questions that will always remain unanswered. We'd entered a world of 'unreality' where normal accepted everyday things such as shopping, what to have for dinner and just getting up, became inter-twinned with all the difficulties associated with a 'sudden traumatic death'...one of my three children was now missing! Never to return!

Issues to confront and deal with such as the Police investigation, the Coroner's Office, the Crown Prosecution Service and its role in the future Trial, the Criminal Justice System, Court Appearances for Bail renewals, Defence Statements and so on! Post Mortems... the long wait to have a funeral service, the weeks that turn to months (in some cases families have even had to wait years before their loved-ones can be released). We waited 3 months for the return of Westley, always with the frustration of knowing that the Defendant(s) has the right to ask for more than one Post-Mortem, which happened in our case.

As a parent, my over-whelming grief made worse by the grief I witnessed the remaining children suffering at the loss of their brother. A monumental tidal wave of helplessness had swept through our home like a Tsunami!

It's the hardest thing in the world, to celebrate a life taken by an act of violence! A life stolen before it's allotted earthy journey...of 'three score year and ten'...

the precious life of a 'loved-one!' It's hard also to think of 'hope' or the future when 'life' has been rendered meaningless through the magnitude of such over-whelming grief!

How could life ever have colour again? How can anyone who experiences this kind of terrible grief remove the 'black' curtain that comes down the day a beloved child…sister, brother, husband or wife is stolen from view by violence 'with malice aforethought?' Or, feel those unseen hands…that seek to try and help guide us through such horror?

It's a long road before 'one' feels normal feelings again but, laughter, light and colour does return…I can attest to the truth of this statement! However, I must add here that even though a number of years' has passed since Westley's murder, I'm still sometimes brought up with a start when a sudden smell, piece of music or even seeing someone that looks like him, triggers the intense grief felt on the day the news was delivered that Westley had been killed. One can never be complacent, these feelings can be revisited, without warning! I am not unique… this is reported in studies by many bereaved victims' families affected of homicide. It is acknowledged that nothing can take away the overwhelming pain. But, in the wake of this grief the family structure is sometimes broken as the personal grief can isolate each member. Many parents (and/or siblings)…at some point have considered suicide and tragically, some have succeeded. Some parents experience marriage breakdown or become unfit to work and lose their home or business. Certainly, many family members have reported suffering subsequent health problems. It is also on record that the premature death of a parent has often been brought about by the intense relentless level of grief experienced. Research also highlights drug and alcohol issues being experienced by family members trying to self-medicate to mask the grief. These are just some of the issues that myself and many other bereaved victims' families have needed to have recognised by government, doctors and psychologists.

As a result of my personal campaign to raise awareness to the problems faced by victims, subsequently met and worked with Sara Payne when she was appointment the Victims' Champion and with the first Victims' Commissioner, Louise Casey CB who produced her Report 'Review into the Needs of Victims Bereaved by Homicide' that highlighted the need for specialised trauma therapy and peer support. Therapy and peer support is now recognised by Government and other support agencies as being necessary to help those families to cope and help learn to find a new normal. With support 'one' does learn to 'accommodate the grief'…it still hurts to one's very soul but, good memories come back quickly to bring comfort again.

Since this happened to Westley I've realised that you don't have to be an extraordinary person to find yourself thrown into an extraordinary set of circumstances! I've also found that I've been truly blessed to meet many extraordinary people during this challenging journey! These inspirational people continue to be a source of strength. In turn I hope I can bring strength to others who may be unfortunate enough to experience this kind of traumatic loss…

I've become very aware that 'Westley' walks with me wherever I am! I pray that all my family and indeed, anyone reading this that has experienced this kind of grief, can allow the spirit and memory of their 'loved-ones' to become...

'The wings beneath their feet...the reason to get up each day...the dawn beyond the darkness. Hope in their hearts for the strength to make change. The wisdom never to seek revenge...to bury anger and join together to benefit Justice! If we cannot benefit directly ourselves to fight on for others to benefit!'

On the days when I have energy to spare I can take the hand of the next person, to help them through. And, I pray that my heart can continue to be full enough to reach out to those families who may be experiencing the trauma of Homicide. In working with hundreds of families over the years' that have been affected in this way, I realise the importance of finding a 'new normal' of finding a sense of well-being, of having compassion and being able to empathise. I try to remember to look to my left and to my right to remind myself that the person next to me, unbeknown to me, may be on the same journey!

Personally, I've learned that 'letting go of the pain and sense of anger'...although, incredibly difficult at times... has made way for treasured memories to return that will always remain!

These warm memories of happy times, funny times... of Christmas' and past birthdays, help to give meaning and purpose to Westley's life! It's wonderful that I can speak about Westley again with the rest of the family without feeling as though I've had a spear plunged into my heart. These happy moments bring 'hope' and 'joy' back into '*our*' lives, in '*his*' memory and much has been achieved to benefit others since he was taken from us.

Westley's life was stolen...during an 'unprovoked attack' at a cash machine, it could have happened to anyone! In fact the Judge in his Summing-up said...

"If this could happen to Westley, it could happen to anyone!" During the Trial of the two brothers responsible, it became evident that they'd both grown up actively involved in violence, the use of 'Knives' and weapons...even making threats to kill a Police Officer only 5 months prior to killing Westley! Shockingly, even this threat did not result in a 'custodial sentence!' These brothers were 31 and 36 years old at the time they committed this terrible crime...their ages struck 'alarm bells!' How serious is the issue of violent crimes involving Knives? What statistically is the correlation between that of Knife Enable Crime to Gun Crime? How could the problem be addressed?

In the early part of 2006 with the support of Sir Bob Russell (Member of Parliament for Colchester) called for a Home Affairs Select Committee Inquiry in to the issue of Knife Crime. My research at that time suggested that the public were 4 times more likely to be involved in a knife incident than a gun incident. Figures, obtained supported this by revealing the fatalities for the previous 9 years...2026 fatal stabbings to 601 fatal shootings!

Neither should be happening on our Streets...Murder in whatever form is wholly unacceptable in a civilised Society. At that time, all too often **'Sentencing' for 'Knife Murder' falling short as both 'Justice for the Victims families' and as a deterrent to the would be 'Criminal Perpetrator!'**

Subsequently, together with Essex Police and other key supporters...submitted a petition of 21,710 signatures to 10 Downing Street and Tabled the House of

Commons on the 12*th* March, 2007 calling for tougher sentences for Knife Crime.

On the 21*st* March, 2007 my personal petition of 5,000 signatures was Tabled in the House of Commons and recorded in Hansard, again in the matter of 'Knife Crime!' However, my personal Petition called for '**Knife Crime**' **Sentencing** to be brought in line with '**Gun Crime**' **Sentencing**: www.KnifeCrimes.Org/Law-Changes-Knife-Crime.html As a result of lobbying for many months during 2006/7 with the support of Sir Bob Russell MP for Colchester finally achieved the 1*st* Home Affairs Select Committee Debate on 'Knife Crime' held on 27*th* March, 2007 calling for 'Knife Crime' to be treated in the same way as 'Gun Crime' when Sentencing as well as a Nationwide Education Programme. My Report in the form of a written Memorandum was submitted (full information and a copy can be accessed from our website www.KnifeCrimes.Org).

I later gave Oral Evidence to the 2*nd* Home Affairs Select Committee on the 20*th* January, 2009 to reiterate the foregoing, resulting in the Review of Section 21 of the Criminal Justice Act 2003 to bring 'Knife Murders' in line with 'Gun Murders' also a National Education Programme to deter young people from crime. This campaign was successful and achieved the 25 year Tariff Review for Knife Murders which took effect from 3*rd* March, 2010.

In memory of Westley the charity Prince of Tides 'Westley Odger' Foundation was founded off the back of an existing charity, formed in 2003. The Charity's working name is KnifeCrimes.Org which has an 'Online Resource' website www.KnifeCrimes.Org The organisation has grown to support hundreds of families, campaigns to improve rights for victims' families and works with Government, along with all 43 Police Forces throughout the United Kingdom. We also work closely with the Homicide & Serious Crime Directorate of Scotland Yard to assist in the continued improvement of Family Liaison Officers' understanding of working with families affected and often traumatised by the murder and/or manslaughter of a close relative. The Charity supports active partnership working and is involved in training Safer Schools Police Officers, Youth Workers and Probation to deliver Westley's Weapons Awareness Preventative Education Programme' in Schools, as well as to young people at risk of offending and raise awareness to the consequences of carrying knives and bladed weapons.

I believe making change is possible in the memory of all our 'loved-ones'...making a stand by joining together to demand change! Victims' families need to have their 'Human Rights' recognised to 'dignify' the loss of their 'loved-ones' and, in so doing, bring about Statutory Rights enshrined in Law! These changes are possible by working collaboratively with victims, victims' organisations and all agencies concerned with Criminal Justice.

As a regular contributor to Media...Radio, TV News, Documentary Film content and Crime Research Reports, I lecture on the subject of Victimology and Post Traumatic Stress (PTSD) in Homicide Victims' Families. On behalf of the Charity I regularly work with the Home Office, Ministry of Justice, Crown Prosecution Service and Scotland Yard in an advisory capacity to further improve victim rights.

I have been incredibly privileged and proud to have had this work in memory of Westley recognised when

I was awarded in the Queen's Birthday Honours 11th June, 2011...to be made a 'Member of the British Empire' for 'Services to the Prevention of Knife Crime'. Lastly, if you're reading this footnote, you've no doubt purchased a copy of this book. It therefore remains for me to say a personal huge 'thank you' for supporting the work of Prince of Tides 'Westley Odger' Foundation. The Charity's Trustees and I are truly grateful.

Anyone affected by murder or manslaughter, who may need some help or advice, please contact us by visiting our resource website www.KnifeCrimes.Org

Author: Ann Oakes-Odger MBE

Lightning Source UK Ltd.
Milton Keynes UK
UKOW02f0059061016

284598UK00001B/29/P